Lingering Tide

and Other Stories

Latha Viswanathan

We acknowledge the support of the Canada Council for the Arts for our publishing program. We also acknowledge support from the Government of Ontario through the Ontario Arts Council.

Cover Design: Ingrid Paulson

Library and Archives Canada Cataloguing in Publication

Viswanathan, Latha
    Lingering tide : and other stories / Latha Viswanathan.

ISBN 978-1-894770-75-0

    I. Title.

PS8643.I885L56 2011   C813'.6   C2011-904557-5

Printed in Canada by Coach House Printing

TSAR Publications
P. O. Box 6996, Station A
Toronto, Ontario M5W 1X7
Canada

www.tsarbooks.com

For my daughter, Ahalya

We shall not cease from exploration
And the end of all our exploring
Will be to arrive where we started
And know the place for the first time.

‿თ

This is the use of memory:
For liberation-- not less of love but expanding
Of love beyond desire and so liberation
From the future as well as the past.

TS ELIOt -- "Little Gidding"

Acknowledgements

My thanks to the Texas Council of the Arts for a Literature Fellowship Grant and to the Sewanee Writers Workshop for a Tennessee Williams Scholarship and a Borchardt Scholarship that helped in the writing of some of these stories.

The following stories have previously appeared as below:

"Lingering Tide" in *Weber Studies*, Vol. 15, No. 1, Winter 1998, Special Issue: South Asian American Literature/Culture.

"Brittle", *Arts & Letters, University of Georgia magazine.*

"Summer Secrets," *Mangrove Magazine*, Volume 3, No. 1, Spring 1996. John Hazard Wildman Prize.

"Eclipse" in *Shenandoah*, Spring 1999. Vol. 49, No. 1, Nominated for Pushcart prize.

"Cool Wedding," Vol. 52, No. 2, *Shenandoah*, 2002. Goodheart Prize for Fiction, 2002. The Year's Best, New Stories from the South, 2003. Nominated for NPR's Selected Shorts program.

"Third Eye," in *Women's Work*, Spring 1997.

"Attar" in *Other Voices*, Vol. 28, Spring/Summer 1998.

"A Couple of Rogues," *Many Mountains Moving*, Seventh Issue, Vol. 3, No. 1, 1996.

An earlier version of "Bat Soup" appeared in *Fiction International*, Special Issue: Pain, No. 29, 1995.

"Traveling," *Crab Orchard Review*, Vol. 9, No. 1, Winter/Spring 2004.

"Bee Mind Lotus Bud" in *StoryQuarterly*, 36, 2000. Nominated for Pushcart Prize.

"Matsutake," *Rattapallax Magazine*, Issue No. 7, 2002.

Contents

Lingering Tide

SIX PM IN BOMBAY IS EARLY morning in New Jersey. The hours Surya struggles to fill in India have yet to be born in America. The telephone rings. His son Prem's voice is solicitous.

"Are you all right? How was the trip?"

"What do you mean all right? I'm here, aren't I? You tell me, how are the children?"

"I just wanted to make sure you reached safe and sound." Prem's tone is controlled and patient, as if addressing an uncomprehending child. "We're okay. I'll call you again soon. Renu will call too."

Too many calls, Surya thinks, to ask about safety. Is anyone really safe? An absurd idea.

All around the apartment, the walls, end tables and coffee table, Uma's face smiles back. Carefully, lovingly, he has plucked her young face from old albums. Everywhere he turns, her face remains frozen, encircled with yesterday's flowers, trapped in black and white photographs.

⁓

It had happened a long way away from home in a place called, of all things, Succasunna, in New Jersey, where his son took care of the details. Prem, an actuary by profession, was an efficient, orderly type. He had made arrangements with a funeral home nearby. They were very organized, he assured his father gently, showing him a pile of documents, certificates, medical reports from the hospital, all of them stamped and signed. His daughter Renu flew in from Vancouver. Son and daughter whispered and hovered around Surya, anticipating all sorts of imagined needs.

The end had been quick, a matter of ten days. By then Uma was incredibly weak, lost in a world Surya couldn't reach. Her only nourishment came from tubes. Surya resorted to a liquid diet. After they pumped her body full of painkillers, she barely spoke to anyone. She became a catatonic creature, moaning with vacant eyes. He communed with her in silence. He stopped writing letters, answering phone calls, talking to the children and grandchildren.

The last few days, Uma's small, shrinking veins turned stubborn. The nurses couldn't pierce her arms. The glucose, the platelets, the blood bags, all these had to find a way. They mapped out a shunt through veins that ran down her legs. When it was all over, Surya slipped out the needles. The skin continued to weep, a red trickle moistening the sheet underneath. The sphincter relaxed; the nurse and he changed her diaper. She was dead and things went on. It had shocked him.

The funeral director had offered Prem many options. There were all sorts of caskets to choose from, depending on what they wanted to spend. Did they want embalming? he asked. When Surya found out what this was, he shook his head. What was the point in puffing up Uma's skin?

During the cremation, he stood by his son. Prem's fingers had trembled as he placed the piece of camphor on his mother's chest. Watching the funeral home people slide her in, Surya thought he saw a kind of relief flicker on their faces. For Uma, an end to meaningless pain. For Surya—what?

∽

A month after Uma's death, Surya's silence continued. The children became worried. They'd thought their father a strong man, obdurate at times, even domineering as a young man, but very much in control, always there. Was this quiet, almost indifferent man, the same man they knew? Startled by the transformation, they conferred, procured invitations from friends, dangled notions of exaggerated importance, the role a grandfather played in children's lives.

For the past few years, he'd watched the grandchildren. They came home from school it seemed only to go out. They were busy miniature adults. They had so many illusions to break. What could he, an old man from another country, offer in the way of enlightenment when it came to ice hockey, baseball and track?

He blended with the evening shadows, sitting in the quiet of his room. Brother and sister were in the kitchen, exchanging holiday plans.

"Camping is great fun for the kids," said Prem, in a studied, deliberate tone.

Renu's trilling voice: "We loved Mexico. Maybe Cozumel this time."

Surya walked towards the window. A summer thunderstorm was beginning outside. A stripe of lightning and a corner came to life, oak branches reaching out. Tails of sphagnum moss tucked tightly into hanging baskets on the patio spilled out, Swami beards, taking him back.

After the rains, he would watch Uma in the terrace garden of their flat. She had stopped weeding and wiped the sticky juice of bruised leaves from her palms. He watched as she balanced a moving clot of soil in her hand. "Isn't it amazing?" she said. "This earthworm, how it tunnels all the time? This garden, I think it's mine, but I'm just somebody puttering for a while . . ." Surely, there, Surya thought, his mind would cling to thoughts of his wife, the way she'd been alive?

He broke the silence. "I want to go home. I want to take her back."

Renu and Prem ranted and raved. They spoke in pious gestures, in between making necessary travel plans. They held onto him while he walked down the stairs, they shushed the kids, turned off the television. Surya gripped the chair, editing sentences before they began, scrunching a fistful of the curtain material hard. It was perfectly natural, he felt, that

3

he'd want to go back. He didn't see the need for any distractions now. He wanted something else. A state where life zigzagged, he was a young and old man, guru and disciple at the same time. Somehow the present always assumed a place of diminished importance in India. Was it the daily assault? The chaos, the mingling of absurd and profound, that fleeting sense of a glimpse, a tip of meaning that surfaced sometimes? He needed this fragile preservation now.

⌒

By his side, on the table, sat an aluminum tin, the remains of his wife. The lid was sealed shut, a protruding coin of red wax on either side. He carried it, feeling the weight of bones and flesh. In the cupboard, he put the container between piles of cotton saris, the ones she couldn't take with her to America. He turned off the lights. In the dark, there was a semblance of comfort, no more groping shuffling thoughts. Like some young, tireless lover, he courted sleep, the escape it offered.

With dawn comes a moment that is still a seed. It carries a core of potential, of promise, the obfuscation gentle on the awakening mind. He felt it envelop him, that delicious boundary between the conscious and unconscious. He longed to prolong it somehow. If he heard no other sound to indicate that the city had come to life, he might manage to string a few such moments together, feign indifference a little longer. It was no use. Behind the eyelids, he felt the day crawl, mouth open wide, imploring his participation. Then the thoughts began. With awareness came the dullness, then sharp pain, losing her yet again as if for the first time.

His daughter called. Surya knew he was lucky. There was no question about his children's devotion. There were times in America when he thought he detected a trace of irritation. Perhaps it was his helplessness. He was a dependent in a foreign place. He made the past in them come alive. A past they'd jettisoned. Did they think he was forlorn, innately pathetic, stuck in the periphery of the world outside? It didn't matter anymore. Despair. Self-pity. These were luxuries for the uninitiated.

The grit on his feet made him look down. Uma's favorite carpet, now heavy with dust. He remembered the day they had ordered it. The family, three generations of carpet weavers, had shown them the drawings, the samples. A sullen eight year old sat in the corner of the room, oblivious to them, working with intense concentration. The children in these families worked as hard as the adults. These carpets needed the skill of small fingers to achieve that level of density, that look. He saw the hands that made the knots. Those cuts, the calluses on small fingers. A childhood lost so family could survive. He heard the father say, "Now remember loop around tight like this so the wool doesn't slant."

The distended cheek, the tongue that worked, helped the boy keep up the pace of his hands. Eyes and fingers would work for weeks. When it was half, no, three quarters done, he'd be reminded it was time to stop, put in a subtle flaw. A thing that proved no machine had touched the job. "A designer signature, a calculated pattern error," Surya had said.

"No," Uma countered, "the child giving of himself, that's what gives the piece life, don't you understand?"

༂

Outside, the stifling heat of the day had begun. The breeze from the sea in the balcony was weak, it did nothing to relieve the humidity in the air. From the apartment above, a nasal voice rose. The call to Allah. The wail, a plaintive cry, hung above him, obliterating all other sounds. On his trip back to India, he'd heard the same cry. It was in London—Heathrow, in fact. He had disembarked and was going down the escalator. Just outside the men's room, tucked in a corner, a man stood facing towards Mecca. He mouthed the words softly. The man struck Surya as wise or completely stupid. Which was it? Was he so powerful that he could lose himself here, accumulating for the life to come? Or was he carrying on with a habit, a sight to be ridiculed?

In the distance, above the Towers of Silence, the dakhmas, he spotted a circle of birds—vultures—buoyant on lazy, warm air. A visual signal from shy scavengers. They patrolled at a height, in anticipation of corpses. Soon alerted by the sudden descent of a neighboring bird, they came from all directions. According to the Avesta, the holy book, to cremate or bury the dead would defile the elements. Parsis offered their bodies to the birds, a final sacrifice.

In the evening, when pedestrians walked by the towers, the tree and the menacing presence of vultures made them walk by faster. There they sat on a big banyan tree with exposed roots that hung down from the branches. The aerial roots reached deep into the ground, offering support for the trunk, feigning an appearance of several trees at a glance. For the vultures, the tree had become a focal point, a waiting ground. The accounts he heard had remarked on the eerie effect produced by the street lights. They said squirming shadows pushed through branches and reached out into passers by. The birds drifted in and out silently, phantoms of the tropical night.

What did they attack first? Surya wondered. The eyes? He imagined the talons resting firmly on some young face while the hooked beak pulled and tore. Rigid pecking order would be observed according to the size of the beak. There would be hissing and clawing while the timid ones sneaked in. He saw the leaders reach in deep with their bald, long neck, making life out of death. The others watched dully, staring through filmy eyes. Upstairs, the wailing ended.

In the evening, Surya sat on the low cement wall by the beach. In a few minutes, the sun would be gone. The sound of the waves was hypnotic. The repetitive pattern: the slow coil of the curl, the stretching, the leveling and spreading with a hiss. Why was he compelled to watch? He was sucked into it, as if in a trance. He would have liked to still the movement, for one incalculable minute. The sea cleansed itself of him continuously.

Years ago, sitting here like this with Prem and Renu, they had seen a beached whale. Trapped in shallow waters, it had stranded itself.

"Why? Why did it do that?" they wanted to know.

He'd told them nobody knew. It remained a cetological mystery.

"Was it lost?" Renu asked.

"Some people think so. They say the sloping beach makes them get lost. They can't hear the other whales." Surya recalled reading that the beach had no surface to echo their sonar waves, the acoustic signals they depended on.

He himself wasn't sure of this. Where else could they strand? He was partial to the theory that the stranded whale had been sick. It had come to the shore not knowing where else to go. Self-preservation would not allow drowning. For an air-breathing mammal, it would be unnatural, horrible. He'd read that they sometimes stranded in great numbers. Surya thought of them traveling in reassuring pods. One sends out a wild distress call and they come, defecating in sympathy. Death became an affirmation of community. It was pure, touching. It moved him.

The children and he returned there the next day. The scientists came. They scraped the algae, carved out the ovaries and counted the ripple marks on the whale's teeth. They also snapped several photographs, probed and peered some more, plopping samples into bottles of alcohol.

Then the vultures came. They squabbled over the carcass near a massive, gaping wound. They stripped and peeled the skin, exposing the insides. After a hot day's sun, the stench had been unbearable.

ᘓᕽ

Surya had been standing in front of Uma's cupboard for a while. Finally, as if he'd just entered the room, he opened the doors in a hurry, the doors swinging back, nicking the paint on the wall. So early in the morning, he knew the beach would be deserted. The man upstairs had finished his wail. The carpet in the living room had been swept. Surya's face was calm as he left the apartment.

He settled himself on the wall. The predatory creatures were here too. The gulls. The crows. And the vultures? Didn't they roost together at night in crags? Then he remembered they had no call. Theirs was a secretive, unseen presence. With dumb, infinite patience, they waited for daytime, when together, they would feed again. Perhaps they'd already left for the dakhmas.

Carrying her ashes, Surya walked towards the waves. They'd been married for forty-five years. Shivering slightly in spite of the heat, he opened the lid and immersed the ashes in the sea. The water soaked his

7

pants; his mind thrashed about, slashing the surface, performing a breach, traveling deep. The images came to him, all jumbled up: the ebbing waves of her body, the weaving child, a crying man, beached whales, the birds—shards of himself that fused and dissolved. This small part, how to hold onto it, make it his lifeline? He heard the rhythmic beat of his heart and felt the dampness cling to his thighs.

Finding his spot on the wall, he sat down. It was high tide. The air was heavy, the monsoons were almost here. When the rains came, he wouldn't come here for several months. The rocks became treacherous, covered with moss. To his right, above the place where the washer-women rinsed their clothes, he thought he heard flapping. The birds were here too. He felt their presence. Together, they watched the waves.

Brittle

FATHER'S DUSTY, OLD, BLACK AMBASSADOR burped to a halt in front of grandmother's house. I wanted to meet Ammini, my friend, the old woman who lived across the street, but I didn't want to face the dragon yet. Ammini was also grandmother's childhood friend. Two summers ago, when I was twelve, Ammini's husband, a bad-tempered man whom I secretly called the dragon, had caught me and Ammini in the kitchen playing house. He flung the miniature vessels, making her cry. I had stuck my tongue out instinctively, making Goddess Kali face, scraping feet on the floor, imitating the shuffly way he walked. I heard Ammini howl. The dragon turned; I froze. By the time I realized he'd left the house, Ammini was gone. I found her in the garden, muttering to her toes, squashing black ants. I retraced my steps and picked up the broken toys, stiff arms of tiny ladles, a cracked wok. Climbing on a wooden stool, I put the toy basket back. The dragon said nothing to Ammini, his wife. He told grandfather I was a high-strung, spoiled child.

తా

I peeked into a window of Ammini's house. The dragon lay on a bare wooden cot, snoring like a speeding scooter. An English mahogany

9

grandfather clock tick-tocked in the background, an absurd accompaniment to the grating sound. I stifled my giggles with the large cotton handkerchief I'd brought to collect gooseberries. A detour through the back, I decided. The dilapidated house had a wild, overgrown garden. This garden was of particular interest to me. Every summer, I collected gooseberries from the bushes in the back so grandmother could make my favorite pickles. I loved sucking the tart fruit till goose bumps raced down my spine. Then I would rush to drink a glass of water to savor the sweet taste.

Before the dragon caught us, Ammini and I spent hours together, playing house. High on a granite shelf, she hid a cushion-like bamboo basket filled with miniature sandstone replicas of grown-up cooking utensils: woks, saucepans, tureens, griddles and minuscule ladles. We prepared elaborate, gourmet feasts. Thick lentil sauces mixed with ground coconut and chilies, roasted baby potatoes, deep fried split pea fritters sprinkled with tangy red onions, ground rice and brown sugar pancakes sizzling in clarified butter, yogurt so thick and rich you could cut it with a knife.

When it came to picking the dishes we made, Ammini had no discrimination. Except for peanut brittle. That was mandatory. "Yes, let's," she'd say, pouncing on every suggestion I made, her glazed eyes doing a dance of desire. Then she divided the unseen portions, one fourth for me, three fourths for herself.

It was the summer after my ninth birthday, when I'd received a new doll.

"Ammini, what about the children?" I asked, glancing at my doll, pink and plastic, decked out in a frilly frock. I adjusted the shoulder folds of a faded checkered towel that substituted for a sari. Ammini's face filled with the benign expression that endeared her to the women in my family, especially my grandmother. I marveled at how her oiled, slicked black hair seemed to stick to her scalp like latex paint. Her skin had a permanent yellow tinge from vigorous use of turmeric. The eyes, with their slightly out-of-focus pupils, wore a filmy, milky sheath. She had a bad case of cataracts. "But, Ammini, what about the children?" I repeated impatiently.

"No children, no, no, no, it's all for me. I'm the child," she smiled, baring her receding gums.

"You're too old to be a child. You've got to be a grown-up," I wailed. She was just a shrunken old woman, all doubled over, always muttering to her toes. I couldn't picture her deformed body, her webbed flat feet, the sheer curtain-covered eyes, as those belonging to that of a child.

"Grown-up? Oh, I play that all the time. Wife, husband . . . pretending for the best . . . I want to throw a tantrum; peanut brittle for dinner, sugarcane juice at tiffin time. Like her," Ammini said. She pointed to her lumpy rag doll, no separate fingers or toes, barely wrapped in a filthy sari, half-torn woolen eyes. She plucked the kitchen towel tucked into her sari pleats and blanketed the doll, lifting it gently, pressing it to her chest. I stared as she rocked back and forth, patting the doll's back as if burping a child.

I approached the center of the garden at the back. Away from the shade of the trees and their spreading canopies was a small vegetable patch. Ammini grew flowers for the dragon's morning prayers in raised beds on either side. Ruby hibiscus, fiery petals drooping like dogs' tongues in the heat, gardenias with their cloying scent, sweet basil, coral firecrackers with a single gold speck in the middle. Early in the morning, heaped high in a filigreed brass basket, Ammini carried the flowers to the main room of the house. The wall was covered with pictures of Gods and Goddesses from Hindu mythology. Lakshmi perched daintily on a pink lotus; pot-bellied Ganesha sat nearby. Shiva danced in blissful ecstasy. Circles of vermilion eyes and sandalwood paste adorned each picture.

From the year I learned to cross the street by myself, I had watched the dragon pray. He chanted his mantras loudly, in typical full-throated, sing-song fashion. The tinkling of the little bell meant that others had to lower their voices, talk in hushed whispers. All of a sudden, "What is for lunch?" he snapped at Ammini. "Has that wretch of a man delivered the two sacks of rice?"

"Yes. Don't worry, I've taken care of it," Ammini said, running to the main room, wiping the sweat off her face with the edge of her crumpled cotton sari. It wasn't considered wifely conduct to speak from the kitchen. She walked briskly back to her cooking. In the kitchen, where it was beastly hot, Ammini threw her head back, tilting a stainless steel tumbler at least four inches from her face, pouring water into her mouth. Her throat made gurgling pigeon noises as she swallowed fast. When I tried this later in Bombay, I poured water all over myself.

"A man needs to know if rice has been delivered. A man needs to know what is going on in his own house," the dragon muttered under his breath. The forgiving Gods waited for a bit while he attended to earthly matters. Renewed by the interlude of trivial information, he plunged deeper into his mantras, his sonorous voice rising into a crescendo, reverberating in the uppermost room in the house. Ammini was frantically busy. Banana flower and jackfruit in woks hissed and sizzled as she scraped coconut, moving frantically to get rice and three vegetable dishes ready for lunch. The dragon refused to wait a single minute after his prayers for lunch. The banana leaf had to be washed and placed in a corner of the main room floor, the wooden *palagai* seat dusted and leaning against the wall, a steaming mound of rice ready and waiting on the leaf so he could make a well for fresh ghee. If lunch was late, he yelled at Ammini, making her cry.

⌇

The well in her backyard was hidden behind pillars of banana stems. Leaning out the kitchen window, last time we played house, I had watched Ammini draw water from the well. Clutching the shiny brass water vessel to her waist like a squirming toddler, she slipped the twisted rope around the rim of the container. It went down, deep down, as she pulled the braided jute towards her heaving chest. The dome-like vessel gurgled, drank deep of the cool liquid. I ran outside. I begged my turn; I tried hard to emulate her style. My soft city hands made the vessel a clumsy, graceless diver; the rope chaffed my skin. Ammini made a chortling noise. I glared at her gums, those familiar pink purple stripes. Then she hugged me, a gesture of consolation.

"Here." She held out a piece of juicy sugarcane.

I shook my head.

"Mmm. Sweet and good," she teased, tossing an imaginary piece into her mouth. "How can a mother of so many children be this stubborn? You're the mother, remember?" I grabbed the sugarcane from her hand. The sweetness raced around my tongue. My grandmother forbade sugarcane in our house, believing it made our tonsils swell. I chewed and chewed till the fiber was a bleached, wrung-out stuck-together bunch of strings in my mouth. Squatting near the washing stone by the well, she chewed as I chewed.

"Tell me a story," I begged. "The one about the mongoose."

I leaned against the washing stone and pressed my knees to my chest.

"Years ago," Ammini began, "long before you were born, there was a mongoose in this garden." The sudden gust of breeze felt good on my face. I watched banana leaves fan like elephant ears. As the story rushed out of her mouth, Ammini's face creased and ironed itself out. I knew the plot well. I told it to myself as she told it to me.

Grandmother, her best friend, was helping her make jasmine strands for her hair. They heard an eerie sound, a mongoose snarl. A cobra had slithered down the bamboo fence. My grandmother put her forefinger to her lips and held Ammini's hand. The cobra swayed its raised hood; the quivering, hissing tongue darted out in a hypnotic wave-like dance. The mongoose bared its teeth with hair bristling at the nape of its neck. Eyes leaking red, he rocked, then traced a circle with his jumps, flying up—down, up—down. The cobra raced after flinging itself—thwack here, thwack again on the ground. With liquid coral eyes, the mongoose flew and saddled the scaly back, riding wildly, being thrown about. For Ammini and grandmother, the moment became so oppressive, it had to burst. The strike was cathartic. The snake lay punched with mongoose teeth marks.

I shuddered; Ammini chortled. "I remember getting up in the middle of the night. That was the time I bled first," she said.

The dolls were napping.

"When I was a girl," Ammini said, "I had peanut brittle every month,

13

on the lucky day before the full moon. I sat near my brother's cradle, holding a cane tray filled with raw peanuts."

I pictured Ammini flipping and tossing the nuts in the air, a Chinese dancer's ribbon, going up with skin, coming down stripped clean. In front of me, her face creased and ironed itself out. Those pink purple stripes widened and came close. I smiled to myself.

"When baby brother fell asleep," Ammini continued, "mother and I slipped into the kitchen. Thick coffee-colored molasses was boiled and seasoned with sweet-smelling cardamom. A cup of water was fetched; a bit of the syrup dropped in. When it congealed into a glistening caramel pearl, the nuts were tossed in. We shaped peanut brittle balls, dancing from the heat on our palms. How we had joked and laughed," Ammini said.

Her mother teased her about her husband to be. "Will you share your sweets with him? Will you let him ply you with store-bought confections?"

The dragon came out, breaking into my reverie, spotted me by the well. "Is that you?" His eyes widened at the way I'd grown. I adjusted my half-sari. "What are you doing there? Go home. Ammini can't see you now." He waved his walking stick at me. "She is tired. Lying down. Wild city child, almost fully grown, still coming and bothering my wife." He hadn't changed a bit. I ran back to grandmother's house.

∽

Every summer, uncles, aunts and cousins, all of us skinny girls, had traveled every summer to this village in Kerala, crowding the old house. In grandmother's house, the noise and crowds of Bombay where I lived with my parents disappeared into some black hole in my adolescent mind. After our final exams, my sister and I filled our suitcases with full-length skirts that reached our ankles, laying aside the pinafores, skirts and dresses we wore the rest of the year. My parents crammed our boxes with educational supplies—assorted books, blank notebooks in case we felt the urge to work.

Fat Goat, my ten-year-old male cousin and his family arrived from

Madras. He followed me everywhere and refused to leave me alone. A whole week passed before I went again to Ammini's house. I remembered the dragon and slouched beside a hibiscus bush. The nearest window was high up, a small rectangular opening that barely lit up the pantry inside. Climbing up the uneven edges of the bricks on the outside wall, I looked inside. There were sacks of rice, wheat, coconuts, pumpkins and gourds, sugar, tamarind, jack fruits, a row of cylindrical stainless steel containers. Like the other houses in the village, anything bought in large quantities was hidden away in the dark of the store room, away from the prying eyes of servants. Some households like Ammini's and ours, put away homemade sweets in steel containers.

Standing on my toes, I grabbed for one of the rusty horizontal bars that striped the window. I thought I saw someone inside. I heard the metallic click of a lid. As my eyes plunged in darkness, I could barely make anything out. I shook my head, sweeping the blurred colored ripples that veiled my vision. The swirling circles dissipated, outlining the familiar hunched silhouette. Ammini was intensely examining a small object in her hands. I stared hard. It was a ball of peanut brittle, about the size of a golf ball. I watched, spellbound. She began to lick it frantically, making frenzied slurping noises. Popping it deftly into her mouth, she closed her eyes in reverie. Rummaging through a corner knot of her sari, she brought out the next one. The ritual began all over again. The close scrutiny, the slurping, the closing of eyes. This was not an opportune time to meet my friend. I was intruding, watching her. The moment felt private.

From grandmother's house across the street, I could hear my cousin shouting my name. That idiotic fat boy. Till he was born, we girls had grandfather to ourselves. I only minded a bit that grandmother plumped up my cousin with extra ghee and curds. Standing on my toes, I heard him call again. I was anxious to meet Ammini, give her my special gift. But I didn't want to be caught here this way.

Back in our house, I cheated and let Fat Goat win at Ludo this time, shut his bleating mouth. When I beat him before at board games, he ran whining to grandfather. I was sorry half an hour later, when grandfather suggested he give Fat Goat swimming lessons. "Grown-up girls from our family don't swim here, you know that," grandfather said when I joined them at the village pond. I watched coconut husks bob up and down, help float chubby arms and legs. I made a face and walked around, enjoying the cool breeze. If I stood facing grandmother's house, the village temple was on the east. To the west was the village pond with murky green water edged with hyacinths and lilies. Elephants, buffaloes and cows bathed here in harmony with village folk. Young men bicycled around the pond in hopes of catching sight of a bare-breasted woman. This rarely happened. Most young women were modest and discreet, they bathed with snug-fitting midriff-length blouses and ankle-length skirts. The water made the cotton blouses and skirts cling like second skin; the men pedaled harder. The veiled view was erotic; you glimpsed at outlines of shape; your imagination filled in the rest.

Grandmother waved to me from the verandah of the house. She went to the temple at this time. I waved back and lingered by the pond, watching a baby elephant. By the time I remembered grandmother and the temple, she had gone ahead. I ended up walking with my aunts, the ones who loved to talk and laugh. They were talking about a plate of barfis they had sent Ammini. "That awful man and that dirty squirrel," they said, "I hope she doesn't share any of it with them." They were talking about the squirrel I had seen last year in a basket.

I had gone to Ammini's backyard, hoping to spend time with her. She was there with the dragon, both of them fussing over something in a basket. I was reluctant to join them but Ammini insisted I come and see what they had. An abandoned baby squirrel nestled in a basket layered with leaves and straw. The dragon fed it milk with an ink dropper, the kind I used at school to fill my fountain pen with Quink ink. Ammini covered her mouth and laughed as the baby drank the milk. After, she took the basket from the dragon and rocked it gently, singing a Malayalam lullaby. They hung the basket on a branch that ran across the kitchen window. Ammini promised to share her peanut brittle as the baby grew big and strong. This was the only time I had seen Ammini and the dragon together that way. I stared at him openmouthed. But he turned away and said to Ammini, "Coffee! Where's my coffee, woman? I want it now."

The temple saw a daily gathering of the faithful, young and old who came there for some air, gossip, and a brief respite from their daily chores. Elderly women like grandmother, heads bowed in reverence, carried small jars of clarified butter, flowers wrapped in starkly veined leaves and tied with banana fiber. Visitors like me were greeted with curiosity and interest. Village women asked, "Where are you from? Whose child are you? Have you begun menstruating?" I shrank back from them, then glared in defiance.

⤵

I came out of the temple and walked back to the pond.

⤵

Fat Goat was swallowing water and struggling. I saw a shuffling figure proceed towards grandfather. Dressed in a filthy dhoti, the dragon's eyes darted everywhere. Aside from his nasty temper, there was this strange walk. He transferred his weight from side to side reminding me of one of our pre-badminton exercises at school.

The dragon's obsession with bodily functions was common knowledge to all. Some fateful mornings, he could be seen swaying back and forth along the front porch, stroking his hairy belly. He agonized loudly over his inability to experience a satisfactory "motion." Bowel movement was, absolutely, the first order of the day. The urge to defecate first was considered supreme; the day could not proceed in disorder. He would not shave, he would not bathe. He cursed at Ammini; he fumed. Passersby on the street were informed of the ailment; they commiserated in earnest horror. This compulsion for evacuation was transferred to neighbors and their descendants. He asked the mothers in our house: "Have they gone today? Have they done their job?" The women never answered him.

⤵

The front door of Ammini's house was open. In spite of the light out-side, inside was cave-like. On the stone shelf in the kitchen, I left Cadbury's chocolate "Nuts and Raisins" arranged in a fancy tin. A squirrel was racing around an open dish of rice. The tin of chocolates was sealed shut, I consoled myself. I glanced up at the topmost shelf. There was the cushion-like bamboo basket with the miniscule cooking utensils. From this angle on the ground, it formed the base of a triangle, cobweb lines growing on the sides, crisscrossing, traveling up to wooden ceiling beams.

I found Ammini way back in the garden, leaning into the well, cover-ing her mouth with her sari, pointing to something inside. "What is it?" I asked, hugging her, then peering into the water. Pink boxes floated everywhere.

"Can't eat like before. Hurts," she said, pointing to her gums. "Let it make the water smell sweet."

"What is it? What's going to make the water smell sweet?"

From inside the house, I heard the dragon's voice. "What's this?" I heard him shout. "Who brought this?" Ammini crossed her eyes and mimicked "Who brought this?" Her fingers pinched a banana stem, then gestured urgently at me to leave. I ran without looking back, taking the roundabout way to our crowded house.

↶∽↷

Grandmother sat spread-eagled on the floor slicing raw plantains to be made into banana chips. "Tell me about Ammini, " I said. Grandmother sighed. "Now that you're grown-up, almost fourteen, I suppose it's time for you to know. If I tell you, you must promise not to bother her. She hasn't been feeling so well."

"What's wrong with her? She's all right?" I asked.

"She's getting old, she tires easily. You understand, don't you?"

I nodded yes. Grandmother sighed again and began to reminisce. Ammini had been a cheerful child. "She was sure to make a great wife," her family said. Married at nine, she came to the dragon's house in the village with festive pomp and fanfare. She chattered and laughed with abandon, played pranks on her doting father-in-law. They played hide and seek in the garden, the old man gasping for breath as he ran. He slipped coins into her palm for shaved ice and syrup. At mealtimes, he placed her little *palagai* next to his. His wife wanted a Calcutta handloom sari like her friend at the next village. His son begged for a cricket set. Father-in-law scolded them both. He said there was no money for their whims. Others in the house watched with pursed mouths, shook their heads. Mother and son cornered Ammini in the garden. Was this proper behavior for a wife? A Hindu daughter-in-law? Grandmother's eyes turned liquid; she dipped her fingers into a bowl of coconut oil to remove the dark stains the peels left behind.

"And then what happened?" I whispered.

"In a year's time, the old man died. With the father-in-law gone, the elders in the house unleashed their pent-up anger. They snatched her toys; they took away all privileges. They drummed wifely sense through a routine of penance. No more sweets. No peanut brittle for you, they said. A Hindu wife learns to shed attachments from her past. She learns to please, prepares to be a mother. Show some respect when we talk, bow your head, drop your eyes where they belong. Scared and nervous, Ammini ran to her husband for help. 'What's a sixteen year old boy to do? He was nicer to you than he ever was to me or my mother,' her husband said, and went to join friends waiting by the pond."

I don't know what my face looked like, but grandmother was silent for a while.

"Months later," grandmother explained, "Ammini came running to me one day all teary-eyed. They were not feeding her properly in that house. All she had was a bit of squash, a piece of pumpkin, watery rasam, rice. After that, I saved treats for her, sweets Ammini knotted into the edge of her sari. She learned to be sly, to eat in secret." Grandmother smiled. "As others in the house slept in the afternoon, she sneaked into the pantry. If they saw her, she told them she had to clean the rice, wipe the shelves, the tamarind pulp had to be dried in the sun. Even later, when she no longer had to, Ammini continued to eat in secret. The pattern could not be broken." I thought of what I had seen, Ammini eating in the dark.

So the years had passed, I found out, with Ammini plotting and deceiving, running to grandmother for an hour of friendship some rare evenings when the elders went out. I pictured grandmother and Ammini stringing jasmine strands, holding hands while the mongoose and cobra fought.

"That was then. We weren't like you city children now," grandmother said. She turned purposeful; slicing, dipping fingers into oil, dropping a pinch of salt and turmeric into the smoking wok. "Grandfather will be returning soon," she said, meaning later, this was no time for talk. Looking at grandmother's face, I guessed the reason to be something else. Perhaps she felt I wasn't ready to hear it all. She was staring into my determined face, raising her eyebrows, recognizing I was serious, that I would pester her relentlessly till I found out.

"I was pregnant with your father at the time," grandmother continued. "Grandfather brought me green mangoes from the fruit vendor. I'd been craving them you know," she said. Embarrassed, I smiled and bit my nail. "I was rubbing mango slices with chili and salt in the kitchen when grandfather said Ammini's husband had not turned up at school. We heard from neighbors he was ill. Grandfather wanted to see for himself but visitors were shooed out of the house. Weeks later, grandfather said his friend had recovered and was back at school.

"Ammini came to visit me one afternoon. We were seeing each other after a long time. She laughed and placed her palms on my hardening, round stomach. How thin and tired she looked, as if she was the one who was ill. She smiled coyly and said the mother-in-law had given them more time."

"For what?" I asked. Grandmother stared as though I were slow. I continued to chew my nails. "Grandchildren. What Ammini must have felt, seeing me swell with child. Then again I did not see Ammini for a long time. I wanted to visit her but her mother-in-law continued to shoo people out of the house. Finally, Ammini came to see me herself. She was sobbing. The dragon couldn't walk normally like before. He shuffled about strangely, dragging his legs. Before the fever, they had been together a few times at night but he ignored her since the illness, refused to touch, calling her an ugly child."

Grandmother shook her head. "What could women like us do? Something must be wrong with Ammini, the word spread. No wonder the poor boy spurned his bride. Isn't it always the woman's fault? When Grandfather came home I repeated what I heard and we fought terribly, calling each other names. He said I should keep out of it. We did not speak for days, it was a whole week before we made up."

Poor Ammini. It was all so unfair. Now that I knew, I hated the dragon even more. How could grandfather talk to him, be his friend? I needed to get out of the crowded house. My sister and cousins were such children, absorbed in tables and sums.

࿊

A fat sweetmeat vendor fanned his wares to shoo away flies that traveled from the animals on the pond. On the mossy stone steps that led to the water sat the dragon. I noticed a bright pink cardboard box from the sweetmeat vendor on his lap. Holding the cheap paper packet tied with a string under his arm, he got up and began shuffling towards the temple. Watching him sway a bit, I wished he'd trip and crack his skull. Running to the fat vendor, I plunked coins from my pocket, practically grabbing the banana leaf packet he handed back. I'd get to Ammini first.

"No sweets now," Ammini said and left the packet on the kitchen counter. I'd forgotten what she'd said, peanut brittle hurt her gums. "Why do you look so sad? Want to play?" she asked, yawning, glancing at the toy vessels. I felt silly, a girl my age, still playing house. But if Ammini wanted to . . . I'd play along . . . I watched her yawn and shake her head, fiddle with the things in the toy basket, count cowrie shells for rice. I hadn't noticed it before, but Ammini's hair looked different, tangled and bushy. No turmeric yellow on her wrinkled facial skin.

"You look different. Are you all right?" I asked.

"You're the mother, I'll be the child. It's baby's nap time," she said. Ammini lay down and covered her face with her sari, falling asleep in minutes, forgetting to pretend. I stared at her for a while then threw a shell in the air, counting, clapping hurriedly before it came down. Could I clap fast like the summer before when I'd counted to eleven? Too bad I was that slow. My fourteen-year-old hands had grown heavy. Even my counting and clapping had not woken her up. I stared at her.

"Get up, Ammini." Her milky eyes twitched, refused to open. I suddenly felt scared. Why was my friend behaving like that?

"I want to sleep. Tired. Go home to grandmother, your Amma and Appa."

Behind me, grandmother had crossed over the threshold of Ammini's house. She spoke in an annoyed voice. "Do as she says. Leave. Go wash your hands and feet and say your prayers. Soon it will be dinner time." Grandmother bent down and pressed a palm to Ammini's forehead. "You rest. Why don't I send a tiffin carrier with food for you and your husband? I'll go see to it now."

I felt a nagging discomfort, things were not going as I planned. Ammini and I had not laughed and talked enough this time. Of all the people in our family, I hoped grandmother would understand. But she was adamant. Walking towards me, she hissed, "Can't you see Ammini needs peace and quiet? No more silly games." I followed grandmother out of the house. I didn't explain that it was Ammini who had suggested that we play house.

‿๑

Fat Goat waited in the verandah, looking very smug. So. He had bleated that I was at her house. I wanted to scare the ghee and curds right out of his stomach. I watched grandmother enter the kitchen, call the other women of the house.

‿๑

I said to Fat Goat in a teasing voice, "I know something you don't know."

"A secret? I won't tell," he promised.

"Come," I said, walking towards the garden, a duplicate of Ammini's backyard. Only grandfather puttered here most days, pruning and clearing, making sure sunlight drenched his lemony pumpkin flowers. "See there?" I pointed to the outhouse. "Behind there is a ghost. The ghost of a cobra that never goes to rest. It waits for someone whose flesh is juicy and plump." I saw that his nose was beginning to sweat, he was standing very still.

"Ghosts don't eat. I know that." His face relaxed, he narrowed his eyes.

"That's what you think. Grandmother says snakes don't attack girls. They only attack boys. Everybody knows that. Haven't you seen your mother join those women near the temple going round the big tree? She's praying to the snake god, saying 'spare my son.' The snake ghost travels all over the village, going everywhere at night. Of course, it never used to come here . . . so many skinny girls. Until . . ." I stopped in midsentence. Pupils fattening like tamarind seeds, he hurried inside.

Fat Goat tattled; and refused to use the outhouse. My parents banned visits to Ammini. They said she was sick; it could be contagious. They consulted with grandfather about a temple tour for us girls. "Culture—history," they said to us. I told Fat Goat I was going to be a swami, grow a third eye.

"I'll open my forehead eye, curse you, and it will all come true. Remember the Mahabharata? Everybody knows the power of a swami's words. My special words are: ashes to enemies, Ludo boards and dice."

"Girls can't be swamis," he said uncertainly, holding his stomach, putting off swimming lessons with grandfather; too much ghee and rice.

෴

Outside the temple in Guruvayur, the first on our itinerary, a woman was selling stuffed cloth dolls. I saw one that looked like Ammini's, only this doll wore a shiny sari, whole buttons for eyes. "Let's buy it for Ammini," I said to grandfather.

"No gifts for anybody this time around. Your parents got them mangoes from Bombay, that is more than enough."

"But please," I persisted, "She has always wanted one like that, I know her better than anybody else."

"No. I have heard enough from you, " grandfather said.

23

"That friend of yours, mean and nasty dragon, he will never get her one." It was too late, I didn't mean to say it out loud. My father squinted at me, my mother shook her head.

"Don't call him that. You rude child," grandfather said. "Grandmother and you think only of Ammini. A man also suffers." The dragon? Suffer? We walked away without buying the doll.

꿍

When we returned to the village from our temple tour, grandmother looked teary-eyed. Ammini was ill with a burning fever. "She's dying," grandmother whispered to the adults.

"I want to go to her," I said. I promised to water the plants in the garden, shell the peas mounded in the straw basket. I even said no to my favorite tiffin.

"Tomorrow," my parents said, "First get a good night's rest. Besides, Ammini needs to be with her husband, her family. Do you think they want neighbor's children about?"

"But . . ." I began. Father gave me that look, the one where he stared without blinking. It began like a staring contest, only this was more serious, I understood. When I played this game with friends, I could outstare the best. But Father always made me turn away. I heard my voice lose sound. Ammini would understand how I felt. The men in my life were almost as bad as the man in her life.

꿍

I woke to a continuous thump on the front door, the sound of wailing from across the road. Everybody in our house was up. Grandfather opened the door. Grandmother looked terrible; hair free and loose, the powdered dot on her forehead smeared into a shapeless stain, eyes and nose red.

"Ammini died in her sleep," she said. I watched her walk around to the back of the house. There she sat on the washing stone by the well. It was time for the cleansing ritual to wash away the contamination of death. The servant maid poured water over her head. I watched grandmother but I was thinking of Ammini. I never got to hold her hand, slip a cowrie shell into her palm for luck. Grandmother was using a towel on her hair. Fat Goat walked up to her and said "Grandfather says the men want coffee."

Before I could stop myself, I shouted, "Why don't you men jump in the well?" Everybody was silent. I yelled it again. "You want coffee? Why don't you men jump in the coffee well?" I was pounding my fists on Fat Goat's chest, my voice all shaky and quivery.

"That's enough. Let the poor boy be," grandmother said.

"What's going on here? What's all the commotion?" Grandfather came out of the house. The women, speeding shadows, exited the backyard and entered the kitchen.

The dragon had sent a messenger to the house. "They want you and the others to prepare her body for cremation," grandfather relayed the message to grandmother.

This time, I didn't wait for permission. I was out the door.

Ammini lay in her lumpy bed on the floor, mouth hanging open like the flap of a purse. Her eyes were rolled back, staring into nothing. My aunts bathed her and sprinkled Ganges water on her body. They shut the stubborn eyelids; tucked a folded cheesecloth-like towel under her chin to close the gaping mouth. It was considered a great blessing for a Hindu woman to die a *sumangali,* a married woman. Young wives trooped into the house and prostrated before the body, asking that they too should be thus blessed. Death had given Ammini special status, a status she never achieved in life.

Grandmother decided to drape Ammini in a red sari. Red was the auspicious color for brides. I was asked to fetch the sari from a trunk in the front room. The corroded little metal box had been part of Ammini's trousseau. Her parents had filled it with toys, rainbow colored skirts scattered with bits of mirror that caught the sunlight and gaudy glass bangles—a little girl's treasures. I noticed a trail of black ants, their circuitous path originating from a small hole in the wall, curving past the dragon's rickety old chair where he sat with his snuff box, into the once shiny suitcase. The dented lid curved out like a swollen lip, making the job easier for the little creatures. Curious, I lifted the lid. The red sari with the gold border lay on top. I tossed it aside impatiently. I was looking for something, I did not know what. I wanted to take a bit of her away from here to the city with me. Underneath her blouses was a suspicious brown lump, wrapped in what had once been a white cotton handkerchief. I lifted the lump and untied the childish knots. Inside were two sickly looking, moldy peanut brittle balls. Dropping the sweets back in the trunk, I grabbed the kerchief and stuffed it into my pocket.

ᴄᴏ

After the usual ten-day mourning period, I entered Ammini's house. In the main room, the Gods with their dots still hung on the wall. The flower basket was empty, the brass bell silent. On the granite shelf, the bamboo cushion squatted, cradled by cobwebs. Outside, the water lay flat in the waiting well; the pink cardboard boxes had traveled, somewhere to the depths. A creature darted in the bushes. I heard a chortle, pictured receding gum stripes.

I felt an urge to peek into the pantry window one more time. Somebody moved inside. The dragon? A muffled sound, then the figure swayed a little. My knuckles jutted like pebbles as I clasped the rusty bars. The dragon was holding something in his hand. He sensed my presence blocking the window light. For a moment, we were still. Then he walked towards me. I saw the squirrel leap onto his shoulder, holding a peanut brittle ball. Through a gap between the corroded bars, the dragon offered me one too, holding out his filthy hand.

"You loved her, didn't you?" he whispered, eyes glistening wet. All I could do was nod my head as I took the peanut brittle from his hand.

Back at grandmother's, I ran upstairs to our family room. I opened the empty kerchief and saw the design. Two brown circles like the outline of a pair of spectacles from moist peanut brittle balls. I placed the dragon's offering in one of the circles and tied the kerchief tightly, placing it behind my pile of books. At dinner, the dragon told grandfather I was a nice young woman, not a high-strung, spoiled child. Father smiled and gave me a look, a soft one this time. It was my turn to be difficult, to look away because I wanted to.

⤳

Upstairs, I watched my cousin lay out his Ludo board on the floor. My sister and he argued about who would be the first to roll the dice. Grandmother had retired early for the night. The men were spending the night with the dragon, a gesture of moral support. The women had congregated on the verandah. I went downstairs and sneaked into the front room. My aunt was whispering what seemed to be an entertaining anecdote. I slouched behind grandfather's massive easy chair.

They were talking about the dragon. "Ever since the fever, I heard from the others, he refused to get close to his wife." Before I could move, my aunt's voice went on. "This is how it must have happened. After the first bout of filariasis, his scrotum, elephantine! His gait turned crooked as he shifted this way and that. Maybe Ammini cried at night because her husband turned away, refused to touch. In the morning, he gave a box of peanut brittle. That would keep her happy for a while."

I remembered Ammini and the dragon laughing and conspiring like children, fussing over a tiny squirrel. Wild laughter ensued from the front verandah. I'll never forgive the women in my family for that. By the time I stumbled upstairs, my sister was doing her victory dance. I cried with Fat Goat. What did it mean to win or lose? It was but a moment. Etched forever in my mind was the memory of Ammini, child to woman, struggling all the time.

Summer Secrets

THIS TIME IT BEGAN before a bath. I closed my eyes. I became a tortured
bride. My mother massaged my scalp with warm oil. The tension had
coiled itself into tight little knots all through my body. Her hands
kneaded my scalp gently, as if probing at first. Seeing my eyelids close,
feeling the stiffness from my skin fall like a robe around my feet, she became more daring and energetic. Her monotonous movements, the
rhythm of her fingers, spoke to me in a way that had been impossible
for her to put into words. She drew circles in my head with her soft, firm
touch. Her helplessness sought mine—she searched for it with demanding hands. Her fingers pinched and trapped the folds of skin on the nape
of my neck. When my mother finished, her hands rested on my shoulder for just a moment.

She placed a tray on my desk—ingredients for my oil bath. Then I
heard the soft click of the door. The dented cups on the tray turned
silver, the oil perfumed with sandalwood, the herbal conditioner: a paste
of coconut milk, peeled aloe and ground hibiscus leaves, a potion of
possibility. It would leave a sheen so bright that my hair would catch the
light. As I removed my pajamas and kurta, sunlight filtered into the
room in a strange pattern. Sieved through the curlicue iron grillwork

that covered the windows, it looked as if a giant web had been tossed into the room. I turned on the radio. Haunting notes of shehnai music filled the air. I sat on a chair in a foetal position with my cheek against my knees and hugged my legs. As the leaves on a branch outside moved gently in the breeze, the light and shadow web swayed around my body. I sat for a while, a giant prey rocking there, feeling the warmth of the sun on my face. Then I stretched my limbs and strolled in for my bath. My hair, now wet and slippery, slithered down my back like a snake. I reached for my breasts and cupped one with my palm. My nipples stood taut. Out of the corner of my eye, I saw a lizard dart in the corner, where the ceiling met the wall.

All through that summer, when I turned fifteen, I felt entwined, grappling with the power of my body, tormented by a new inner life. The thing I enjoyed most that year in school was drama. Now I spent the afternoons reliving movies, reading steamy novels, an occasional Life Science book (I was interested in plants and insects and fancied myself a botanist or zoologist of some kind) and listened to mournful songs.

Summer was a time for weddings and we had our fair share of invitations. During the receptions, I noticed some men and women huddled in corners, sharing gossip about last year's brides and grooms. I heard about beautiful brides now mired in unhappy lives. These stories made me gnash my teeth. I felt, surely, there must be a choice. Why couldn't these women do something—anything—weave an imaginative fight on their own behalf ? If it were me, I'd find a way.

೧

It was April and I was through with my final exams. Summer holidays were a bore in this family, I thought. My friends were away having adventures in big cities. My sister Priya, who was seven, was pulling clusters of oleanders to be made into strands. Here I was, stuck in a sleepy little place, with two middle-aged dolts and a tiresome, whining brat. I glanced at the book I'd been reading last night. It was called *The Strange Lives of Familiar Insects.* I looked out the window into the front garden. We lived in an old bungalow in Coimbatore, a town in South India. My mother was in the kitchen, preparing a tray for my father. I knew the routine well. When it was ready, she would roll the morning newspaper, insert it in the crook of her arm, cover the tray with an embroidered cloth, go to the room where he lay sick, and stay there for an hour. My father, the doctor, had become a patient himself. He had contracted hepatitis and become fragile.

My mother and sister knocked on the door. Priya squealed: her grubby little hands couldn't wait to examine the fiery nail polish bottle on my desk. "Stop that," I said, slapping her wrist.

"What are you doing? Still in your pajamas? Comb your hair, change your clothes," my mother scolded. I shuddered and hoped I'd never be like her. I couldn't imagine being so sour, leading such a pathetic life.

I was glad when they left. I began to daydream again. Standing before the mirror in my room, I applied kohl to my eyes. I dipped a finger into a peacock-shaped jar of vermilion dusted with gold specks and pressed a circle to the middle of my forehead. Diamonds and rubies winked from my ears. I draped myself in a rich russet sari and slid bangles onto my slender wrists. I wound a strand of rice-like pearls around my neck. If I was forced to marry like those brides I heard about, I would weave a clever plan. I was different from them, not so malleable after all. No man was going to mould me to fit some outdated idea lurking in his head.

My sister was kicking the door. I was in the middle of something important, couldn't anyone understand? "Amma says to wash your clothes and get ready fast. Mohan uncle is coming from Madras . . ." I opened the door and pushed my sister out before she finished her sentence.

﹏

I washed my clothes, wrung them dry. I carried the bucket upstairs, to the terrace outside. I passed through my father's dispensary, now silent and unused. It was only a few weeks ago that the place had been full of patients, waiting their turn. Miniature bottles in the shelves stood neglected, still half filled, with tiny, sugary globules, offering homeopathic

cure. My mother turned zealous, a stoic caretaker, forbidding us to go
near him or simply stay and chat.

"He needs his rest; go to your room," she said. "I don't want more patients in this house." I looked at my mother and thought it was a shame.
If it were me, if my husband lay ill, crumpled like a drooping sunflower,
I'd be like Garbo, Meena kumari; I'd suffer in style. When I walked down
our street, I managed to capture a far-off mood. I didn't hear the neighborhood boys whistle and make comments. If, by some remote chance,
their eyes caught mine, I arched my neck, made my face float by.

My mother's brother, Mohan, a chartered accountant, was in town
on business. He came with his friend Rajan, one of the boarders in his
house. The other boarder was Nikhil, "a smart Punjabi fellow," my uncle
said. Rajan was also an accountant. They worked in the same office. All
the time I was telling my uncle about my exams, dance class, music lessons and my friends, I kept stealing a look at this new strange man. He
was a plump and homely type, with a perennially serious look. His fingernails were long and grimy, his clothes looked wrinkled, and he answered my mother's questions in a rapid, sing-song fashion. When he
agreed with what my uncle was saying, I noticed he shook his head vig-
orously, a bobbing apple, I thought. He was definitely not my type.

Just as I was getting up to leave, our neighbor's son ran into the yard.
Priya had fallen off her bike and skinned her knees raw. Rajan ran after
the skinny brat, picked up Priya in his arms, and by the time I returned
with a roll of cotton and gentian violet, she was smiling and joking,
sucking a mint Rajan had popped in her mouth. Perhaps there was a
small streak of kindness in the man but that didn't make up for all that
he lacked.

My uncle said they were leaving in a week. I approached my mother
with a plan. "Let me go back with him to Madras," I begged. "I'll help
aunt with the baby, anything, please—just let me go."

"Oh, all right," she sighed. "You know Mohan travels a lot. Try to be
understanding; put a stop to those moods."

∽

That evening, the cloying scent of gardenias filled my room. Outside the windows, three overgrown bushes were in bloom. I reached out through the grillwork to pluck a flower. I stared. I had spotted a praying mantis, that elusive creature of a single summer. It climbed slowly, taking care to keep its undersides hidden. Once it reached the flowers, it turned to display the plates of color, glistening and waxy like the petals of her neighbors. It remained in the pious pose, motionless, voiceless, waiting for a victim to land. I remembered Rajan. The bush turned fuzzy; my mind dreamt on.

I left his bed on our wedding night. The petals on my side of the bed remained uncrushed. I stood there in my bridal sari, my silver toe rings, the vermilion and turmeric stained thread still golden around my neck. My aunts had dressed up the room for our first night. Over the bed hung a canopy of garlands made from tuberoses and lilies. Rajan tossed and turned all night. I could feel his restlessness, his yearning, drift like a shadow to the floor where I lay. His pain and mine enveloped the room. The silence choked, heavy and dull, an omen of many nights to come.

I remembered a night many weeks ago when I stayed up late studying for my history exam. During one of my many five-minute breaks, I stood before the mirror in my room. The rain outside had stopped. When the last lizard had yelped, the final frog gurgled, and there was no sound, the moment became mine alone. I had felt the clarity sharp and piercing. As I looked at my reflection, I recalled that moment. I turned from side to side and viewed my profile. I was a sculpture in a temple. If I shed a tear, it would travel down the soft mounds of my cheeks, quiver ever so slightly at my chin, make a leap to the tip of my breast, slide and be released, still a whole drop. "He will not know this," I said out loud. The ripples of anger had been temporarily stilled. I had found a way, designed my very own plan.

Like the mantis, I attacked him at the same spot, our bedroom, night after night. I split our bed, building a wall with pillows. If he came close, flung an arm over the wall in sleep, I cried out. I watched the pain tear at his face. Some unguarded moments, he became vulnerable again. He reached out with a smile, a gesture, a pat on the back. I reacted fast. Fool that he was, he had mistaken me for a wife. He didn't understand that our marriage, that farce of supplication, was a plan on my part. I had walked in, arms raised in greeting, a garland in my hands. I had blended in with expectations. I had cloaked my alertness, my combative nature, with a clever disguise. When I caught the lust in his eyes, I waited patiently, cunning in my heart.

The man I really married, I thought, wanted a spirited woman like myself. This sensitive person and I would be above the world, yet with it, always ready to help and empathize. Together, we would dismiss the boring, practical aspects of life. He would be reasonably good looking, not better looking than me, converse in many languages, not give a damn what people thought. Above all, he would understand me from the inside out, but not too closely, a woman likes to keep some unpredictability, certain parts for herself.

I was getting impatient. My lover remained amorphous, faceless, not a real man. The fantasies left me yearning. The boys I knew were all wrong. They gawked and shoved each other in the ribs. They had no idea what passion was. If only I'd known I had Nikhil waiting for me in Madras.

౸

Two weeks had passed in my uncle's house by the sea. I was sorry he had to leave again, this time for Bombay. Too bad Rajan wasn't going with him, I thought. He'd been moping around, eyes watering from hay fever. Rajan and Nikhil occupied the rooms upstairs. Compared to Rajan, Nikhil was altogether different. An intense, artistic sort, he loved music, was easily charmed, and charming in turn. He quoted Urdu couplets, dressed flashily, rode a scooter, and worked as an art director in an ad agency called Lintas. When we met, he smiled and shook my hand with interest, unlike Rajan who had mumbled a weak hello. Finally, I thought, I'd met a real man. True, I was a mere girl and he a grown man, but being mature like I was, I'd always preferred the older type.

The two fellows came down for breakfast and dinner since they helped pay for the cook. These days, it wasn't unusual to find me up and about early, all dressed up. My aunt was alternately feeding the baby or napping, so I was at loose ends most of the time. I borrowed my aunt's card and went to the library twice a week. I borrowed books on etiquette, magazines full of articles like "How to make the most of your crowning glory." I abandoned drinking milk in favor of heavily spiced tea (Nikhil only drank tea); learned how to eat daintily, blotting my lips ever so slightly with a napkin; and always said no to a second helping.

❦

It was one morning after breakfast that Nikhil had asked. He had two tickets for a sitar recital by Amar Khan. Would I like to go? Fighting to control my excitement, I said, "Of course. I adore Amar Khan."

Since I didn't yet own saris of my own, I borrowed two of aunt's, even though she raised her eyebrows quizzically and laughed when I asked. I thought it sad that she smelled of burping washcloths and formula. She'd struck me as such a romantic sort when I'd seen her as a bride. Now she wore her saris above her navel, in case her stretch marks showed. Then and there I knew I'd never let one of those things grow inside me.

After Rajan and Nikhil went to work, I sneaked upstairs and looked around. Rajan's room was bare. There was a metal cot, a hastily made bed, several books with titles like *Small Companies and Taxation, Managerial Accounting, Industrial Psychology* and *How to Read Financial Statements*. The teeth of his comb still shone from the hair oil he used. I shrugged my shoulders in disdain and went to Nikhil's room next door.

The contrast was stark. Nikhil had taken care with decorating. On his walls were Mogul miniature prints. There was a macramé hanger with a wandering jew in the corner by the window, bottles of after shave in a circle on his desk, a bulging bamboo magazine rack by the bed, bookshelves filled with poetry, tapes and records, and a bean bag still dented from his presence, a packet of Rothmans on the stool beside. The bed was covered with a satiny bedspread in maroon. In the middle of the bed, there was a large batik silhouette of a shapely woman. I filled in the outline of her body with mine. I turned to my side. On his bedside

34

table, next to the lamp, stood a framed photograph. A young woman with shoulder-length hair smiled boldly into the camera.

༄

I sneaked down just as quietly as I'd gone up, and went into my aunt's room. She was changing the baby. I tried hard not to look. "Does Nikhil have a girlfriend, anyone special?" I asked, trying to sound nonchalant.

"Nikhil? I guess so. He's known this girl Shalini for a while. But I haven't seen them together, in oh, maybe six months. Why do you ask?" She proceeded to give the baby a sponge bath. She cooed and tickled, and the baby spat out milk. "Just curious," I said. I stole another close look at the photograph. The very next day, I went to the hairdresser.

"Are you sure?" the anxious woman asked. I undid my heavy braid he weight of which had become more than I could bear. She snipped gently at first, her scissors making brief, crisp sounds. My hair fell in dark wisps around her shuffling feet. As she moved up and the thickness increased, my hair flew down faster, unraveling, bits off shiny skeins. When it was finished, I looked down for the last time. A silent gasp escaped from my mouth. Then I looked up into the mirror and smiled at the face that looked back.

༄

The auditorium lights had dimmed. The ustad, a master musician, supported the elongated fretted neck of the sitar, a dying swan in his hands. The polished head, a hollow gourd, wore an ivory colored frieze, interspersed with splashes of color. His fingers strummed the playing strings, the untouched ones vibrated sympathetically. I drifted with the music. I felt the air, the walls, sway to the sound. The plaintive song, Nikhil's hands on the armrest next to mine, I was lost.

The prelude of the next piece began languorously. Each note hung distinct and separate, trembling drops in the air. Now the melody took over. The notes rushed out and mingled, skipping along, ascending and descending in succession. I bit my lower lip hard. As the tempo quickened, I caught Nikhil's profile out of the corner of my eye. He sat there absorbed, his chin resting in his palm. His expression was intense. I knew that he was lost.

The crescendo came, a deafening waterfall. I felt a tingle that made me quiver, traveling all the way down to the base of my spine. I was clawing my way through the frenzied, frantic pace. I felt myself rise and fall. Then the piece was over and the applause began. I had been clutching the pleats of my sari with such force that creases had formed. I felt damp circles spread underneath my arms. Nikhil turned and said, "Wasn't that great, wonderful?" I nodded mutely, words tangled up inside. All through the ride home, we didn't exchange a word. Outside my door, he flashed a crooked smile. If he stepped in, if we were to touch, I'd tug at my sari, slink into my bed. Only this time, I thought, my grip would be liquid, the soothsayer, the virgin no more.

I overslept the next morning, exhausted from the previous night. My aunt was in the kitchen, sterilizing bottles in a pan. She dipped the tongs into the kettle, then lifted the bottles carefully, as if she were in a lab. I poured myself a cup of tea and pretended to read the headlines. A few moments later, Nikhil came down, handsome and dashing in white, a cricket bowler with tousled hair. "Going somewhere?" I asked slowly.

Before he could reply, there was a knock on the door. In walked a willowy woman in blue, a delphinium of some kind. The end of her sari hung to her knees. She looked at Nikhil like she'd gobble him up with her eyes. So this is Shalini, his friend, I thought. My fingers felt icy, my stomach did a hop. She didn't move from her spot near the door, she tilted her head slightly, smiled at me and my aunt, and attached herself to Nikhil, with fingers like vines. I watched them leave, the rend inside engulfing, wave-like. Shalini hoisted herself beside Nikhil, a perfect pillion rider. They sped off in a haze of white and blue, her sari flowing in the breeze. I remembered Vanessa Redgrave playing Isadora Duncan; I hoped Shalini choked on her sari and died.

ᥫᦁ

My holiday was ruined, maybe even my life. I moved about mechanically, a robot, numb inside. Rajan hadn't come down, he had had a rough night. Nikhil had said he was still sniffling and sneezing from hay fever, eyes puffed up and ready to cry. I offered to take up a tray. I dragged my feet up the stairs, put the tray down and pushed the door.

Rajan was kneeling on the floor making muffled sounds. An indigo bottle of Vicks VapoRub lay on its side next to him. He was weeping softly, his face in his hands. His papers were in disarray, all over the floor. His paunch was rippling up and down like he had the hiccups. I could picture it in my mind. Like Ingrid Bergman in Africa, I'd nurse him back to health. What if I walked towards him and placed a palm on his oily, wavy hair? Next thing I know we'd be clinging to each other, like lovers, after yet another spat.

I looked at him. His eyes bore into mine, gimlet thrusts, making me yield. He thanked me for the tray and began collecting his papers. Settling down to work, he turned to me and said, "Are you having a good holiday? It's been nice having you here." At the doorway, I turned and looked at him again. Rajan had dismissed me like a child.

The summer ended and school began. My friends remained adolescent, giggling and spilling secrets. I said nothing. I understood that such things were for feeling, not for sharing.

Eclipse

SHARMA BEGAN THIS SATURDAY like everyday, prostrating at sunrise. Standing, he exhaled and folded forward into an inverted V shape, sliding palms on the floor. Blood rushed to his head. Inhaling, he pushed the left leg back, knee touching the woolen rug pile. The other knee moved to his chest, jutting out from under his right armpit. He arched his back and gazed up, chin towards the light leaking east from the sky. This yogic maneuver involved twelve positions, pulling and loosening his body, cracking the knuckles of his mind.

Later, sandals flapping, he walked to the study, picked up his flute. The turning of pages was followed by trilling sounds. The haunting notes of a morning raga swirled out. As he played, he saw that the mirror on the wall trapped his face, the blatantly receding hairline giving him an avuncular air. During his first year as Professor of Indian music at York university in Toronto, "We will listen to Carnatic and Hindustani classical music," he said to his students, "Not hippie-Beatles stuff." Then, the sallow cheeks had shown a smattering of age spots. Since his fiftieth birthday this past winter, he noticed they spread downwards, encircling the neck, reaching out to fill in gaps. At this mid-point in his life, he felt split between the past and present, between India and Canada, a feeling his wife and son did not share. A husband. A father. How the roles overwhelmed. Divya, still lively, by the time night arrived; Gopal, always in a hurry, shutting Sharma out. He slid back in the chair and continued to play.

The competing whistle of the kettle in the kitchen meant Divya was up. Nocturnal by nature, she usually buried herself behind the paper, acknowledging her anti-social morning mood. A few more cups of tea, the business section read, he imagined her looking up and staring out. Perhaps she admired the crocuses that had pushed themselves up through the night, emerging with purple heads closed, above layers of mulch topped with a dusting of snow. A memory of her face in sleep, that lost look as she curved into the fetal position, floated behind his eyes. For the past three years, Divya had taken evening classes in computer science. She said the investment company where she worked promoted from within, it was important to keep up.

He had finished practicing, shut the study door.

Walking up the stairs, peeking in, he saw that Gopal continued to sleep. Next to the CD on the desk, a pair of socks lay beside the paper face of the American jazz flutist Hubert Laws. The open first drawer of the dresser showed Gopal's birthday present from Divya, a metal flute resting in its box. Beyond this, underneath briefs, was the wooden Indian flute Sharma had chosen for his son, wrapped in a plastic bag.

Five years back in Madras, when Gopal was ten, during one of Sharma's numerous concerts, mother and son pleaded, Sharma relented and let Gopal play a piece. The boy's flute seduced with the charm of a beginner, who, bungling till yesterday, has discovered a secret and flaunts his delight. Divya and Gopal couldn't understand why Sharma had said it was too soon, there was plenty of time. He did not tell them that Gopal played without subtleties, not having lived enough.

The boy had charmed and flirted: "In the middle of doing homework last month, I got distracted and wandered off. My mother lifted me by the ear, pulling me back." The audience tittered and clapped. He spoke endearingly, a soft soprano voice. "I carried my mother's face, her hands on her hips, all through the day. Out of that came my piece, titled *Conversation of Crabs*." Sitting in the half-lotus position when he played,

Gopal kept beat by tapping a knee. On his face, his black pupils danced this way and that, dilating and shrinking when he hit the high notes. Sharma saw the lush curls on his head. The women noticed the ears of his pockets, floppy puppy ears, peeping out on either side. The boy was, unquestionably, an adorable child.

Since they had arrived in Toronto, Gopal opted for lessons in western classical; he also listened to jazz all the time. An amateur musician herself, Divya had wonderful instincts. She knew what was marketable, what people liked. She arranged for Gopal to play jazz on Canada Day at Coronation Park. Was this the North American way, Sharma wondered, not worrying about subtleties, going for rashness, pushing a novice to perform?

⌒

"I'm going for a walk, the usual round," Sharma said to Gopal, stepping onto the white floor of the foyer, Divya's latest project, new ceramic tiles. Zipping up his windbreaker, Sharma left the house. After six years here, he still reveled in the novelty of the world outside. He heard the cardinals on the pine, not raucous crows on tamarind trees as in Madras. In winter he stared at angry stalactites growing from the eaves. He waited to see them melt. They remained sharp and stubborn for days, opaque in the morning sun. The cedar hedge in front of his house had grown too tall. The top growth was scraggly, the stems below too thick.

Divya was raking the lawn. She was always the first one on the street to begin work in the garden, reminding the rest of them to leave winter behind. When they moved to the house in Oakville, she, ill with strep throat, had watched Sharma from the window. He stood humming under the trees, the rake a wooden extension of his hand. He looked up, their eyes met, there was exasperation on her face. He had been flustered by it, the rawness of her look. She had caught him the moment he entered himself, combing the same patch of grass, over and over. Later, when he went inside, "You don't have to be so delicate about it, leaving pine needles behind," she snapped.

"I'm going for a walk, the usual round," he repeated to Divya working outside. He saw that she smiled to herself. The smile evaporated as she surveyed the lawn. "Can you finish the backyard when you come back?"

"I'm working on a new piece. I'll get it done . . . ," he muttered. She frowned. Perhaps she didn't hear him at all. Divya knew how it was when he was working on a new piece. Such things could wait. Leaves belonged on grass, anyway, not squished in plastic bags. Everything had to be immediate for her, as if life was always urgent. "Imagine, a few more weeks and it's music festival time in Madras," he spoke out loud. She worked furiously, drawing lines in the soil under the trees, maiming pine cones that lay in her path.

Turning towards the pavement, he glanced back. There was a time when she said his droopy eyes, the glitter of a chain along the curve of his neck, quickened her lust. Now he felt her eyes zoom in on him, resting on accordion chins, seeing only flab.

He walked down Bronte Street towards the harbor. From there, it was possible to get a good view of the old lighthouse. As he walked there in the mornings, he thought about the absurdity of his presence, the strangeness of it. The wide spaces, the empty streets, the reincarnating gardens, all these things overwhelmed. "But where are all the people?" he'd asked first, when the real estate agent had shown them around. She had been perplexed by his question. Remembering, he laughed at himself.

The derelict lighthouse was no longer used. But Sharma liked to look, to take in the character of it. He saw a keeper with a leathery, weather-beaten face, guiding boats and ships. Walking past the shops which dotted Lakeshore Road, he remembered his brother's remark, a visitor's strange observation. "Isn't it odd? I've never seen so much of the sky at one time." Like Sharma, he too had been overwhelmed. The sky went on and on because you looked up easily, dreamed more. The country felt new, in spite of native Indians and pioneers one read about. The feeling was one of emptiness, the outlines of the houses fuzzy in the fog of the distance, young dreams that clung tenuously, defying definition, dissolving somewhere in the horizon of the eye. As Sharma gazed again and again at the abandoned lighthouse, he smelled the trapped air inside.

41

In the office at the university, he sat among the familiar: old books, the predictable faces of his colleagues; Reinhart and Waddington, the students dashing about outside. These were things that gave shape to his day, the hours stretching before purposefully, filled with classes, things to cross out as done or jot down again under those to come. He was preparing for Introduction to Indian Music class.

Reinhart had stopped him in the corridor last week and asked "Sharma, how about joining our old timers cricket team? It'll give us a good reason to down a few pints at the pub. If you have to think about it, you better think fast."

Sharma had had a ready reply, a kind of dithyramb. "I loathe team sports. The very idea of it. All that rubbish about team spirit. Like children, afraid to be alone. I like to be by myself. I only do yoga and walk."

Surprised by the sudden passion, Reinhart had coughed into his fist.

Through the years, the students came and went, a succession of favored transients. They entered with yearning. Such hopes. Such ambition. With them he became relaxed, whole again. He cherished the role of the intellectual; their cheerful bleached faces, their ideas, it was all part of the esoteric reality that wrapped snugly round as he sat. He would teach them something new, how to appreciate the contours of a raga. When they trooped out at the end of the semester, they'd feel they were moving onto grander things.

At night in his study, Sharma's scattered ideas assumed a different life, as if mocking the hours of daytime. He relived old concerts in Madras as he played; the setting came alive in his mind. Loudspeakers sprouted from trees outside where cooks pitched tents to feed hungry crowds. Bits of banana leaves, ubiquitous Indian plates, piled into mounds, a snack for wandering cows. Since schools were closed for the December holidays, swarms of squealing children ran around adults. When the concerts began they were dragged inside; they sulked and fidgeted before falling asleep.

Reviewers glided in, settling into the few reserved seats. Their eyes narrowed with that derision that comes to critics so easily. The accompanists came onto the stage, followed by Sharma, a spartan and dignified figure in white, carrying his wooden flute. It was a tradition that he set the high standards for others to match. Divya sat in the front row. He had honed each piece, each subtle phrase, infusing the links with brilliance. When he played the song, it was as if he'd flung a veil over the audience, trapping the intensity.

Towards the end of this reverie, Sharma's nerves deteriorated. He replayed later concerts in his mind, seeing those at the back leave gaping seats, fickle neophytes all, clutching tickling throats, clasping weepy infants. Divya had said it was a sign of the times. "Who understands popular taste? They only want the light stuff," she consoled.

A sudden draft slapped from the wooden framed window of his study, caulking dry and cracked. Feeling the chill on his face and hands, he remembered Divya's suggestion, sliding aluminum ones, less maintenance and all that.

ᴄ∽

In the bedroom, she massaged cream into her cheeks, lifting skin, pushing fingers towards lobes. He saw the bare neck. On weekdays, Divya didn't wear the mangalsutra, putting it away in a velvet box among bottles and jars. She said the traditional wedding necklace clashed with her office clothes, the skirts and pants. Seeing her like this, bare-necked with her pastel nightshirt, hair cascading to her waist, there was a moment he felt he didn't know her at all.

Last December, on the morning of the department Christmas party, Divya complained that she didn't feel like going, she had nothing suitable to wear. "What about a sari? You know it suits you best. You look so elegant, your face with a tikka always lights up," he coaxed, just as he did every year.

Five years in Canada and she mumbled that she'd felt uncomfortable in a sari, overdressed somehow. "The blaring colors of my kanjeevuram saris. One doesn't want to stand out like that. Anyway, the heels on my boots pull the gold thread of the border at the back." Sharma couldn't come up with a suitable reply. For her, he thought, there was no need to declare the difference. She wanted to make her Indianness invisible, carry it quietly somehow. The old habits, they had lost their resonance. The past —evanescent and looming with its ghosts and rituals were fragile anchors for her and Gopal. If some corner of Sharma's mind said that was all he had in the end, he would retort but it was me, I chose to abandon it for this reality. Back then it had been easy to envision that they would be a bigger family, bigger than before. Opportunities, financial security, he stacked a nice pile. How was he to know that change might become a habit for Divya, her core attached to ambitions, titillating distractions?

Holding the cream jar, she talked and jolted him out of his thoughts. "Have you thought about what we discussed last night?"

"What?" It came out just like that, before he could edit himself, his blank look telling her he was lost.

"We talked about a Prius. Remember?" He heard the serrated edge in her voice, saw that she scrunched up her brow.

"I thought we'd look into leasing for a few months. What do you feel?" Before he was ready to reply, she continued. "We must have two reliable cars." That edge again. The used Rabbit he drove was giving trouble, it was not economical to pour money into it, she had warned from the beginning.

"Leasing? I don't know . . . Let's think about that."

She turned her back to him and grabbed the lid of the moisturizer's jar. He saw that she screwed it tight, tighter still. Perhaps his words turned her skin into membrane, his affectation, this vague talk, this talk about thinking, like a musical bis she heard too often. I must think about it. Let's think it over, shall we? Yes, I must think about it. In the end, this thinking, was that enough for a woman like his wife?

"There may even be a way to write off the cost in our taxes," she shaped ramifications out loud.

He knew better than to open his mouth now.

In bed he lay still, possessed by phrases of forgotten songs. Divya reached for his drooping center, seeking tumescence every night. He wondered if in her dreams she lay not under but over him. At forty, she was just ripening. For Sharma, when they married, the age difference, ten years, it had seemed irrelevant, a number, nothing else. Now the years between them multiplied, gaping and looming large. He had not expected this, the language changing between them.

~

Once a month, Sharma performed at a patron's palatial house in Erin Mills. He fussed over his clothes, pulling on a silk kurta, buttons of gold, gifts from the faithful of the past. His audience was waiting for him. He felt his eyes sweep the room catching familiar faces, lingering over new. Did they understand the weight of privilege conferred on them? His listeners were an exclusive lot. They came to hear intricacies unfold, capture nuances of profound thought.

The patron's wife walked towards him holding out a gleaming tray. He acknowledged her with a nod and picked up the offering, a glass of fresh fruit juice. Her downcast face made her more alluring. There were numerous older faces, female faces. The patron, a benign man, leaned over and whispered something about the husbands and children, about a tennis match on TV. Settling down on the thick carpets, the women pushed themselves up front. Watching him, their murmurs became muffled. They were silent, expectant faces.

He saw that Divya tilted her head as she caught snippets of conversation from the kitchen. "Really, this place is a little India now. Except for the weather." The woman laughed loudly, admiring her own wit. Another voice, more enthusiastic, said breathlessly, "Sunkist Market sells everything, even bitter gourd. In the winter, I fry it in the garage." Divya swallowed a smile. He knew that look. She saw an image of the woman in a soiled ski jacket, slaving over a smoking wok while the wind howled outside. The gnawing began. A part of him would use it as he played. Was it only with these women that he could be a man?

Later in the car, Divya snickered and said those people were a little mad, their life was illusion. "Did you hear them talk about the eclipse next week? Rahu, the demon, swallowing the sun and the moon? In

Bombay, while I was growing up, we threw old clothes from balconies to beggars on the street. I knew vaguely it was the idea of pollution or something like that. I chose to ignore it. I believed it was a nice way to promote charity. Demons and calamity! Why can't people let go? I think it's because they're scared. All that rubbish, it's a feeling of false security, a way to hold on to who they were. But we're here, you know, the present is important."

Sharma said nothing, perhaps she did not expect a reply.

☙

After dinner one evening, when he finished practicing the new piece in his study, Sharma heard Divya laugh upstairs in Gopal's room. He put away the flute and went up the stairs. She was picking up balled T-shirts from the floor, complaining about the room, pointing to the waste paper basket swelling with wrappers and banana peels. Gopal wore jeans with patches and tears that showed gangly legs. Bulky sneakers made his feet look gigantic.

"Okay, Mom. Don't get mad," he cajoled. "I'll clean up." He had sliced the top of a Styrofoam ball to use as an animal cell for science class. He squirted the Bristol board with the glue gun in his hand.

"You have to lug this around from class to class?" she asked.

"Recess will be longer next Monday," he announced. "We have special assembly behind the gym so we can watch the eclipse for Mr Potemra's class. I'll have time to go to the locker before science."

A conspiratorial laugh, "More time to goof off," she said.

"Mom, remember what we said about fusion." Gopal pointed a finger, it froze in mid-air.

Divya said "Okay," imitating his gesture, pointing back.

Their fingers seemed to activate some invisible wiring. How easily she took up from where Gopal had left off.

Sharma rested his palm on his son's back. "Gopal, I found a magazine article where Rampal talks about Indian music. It's in the study. Would you like to see it?"

Clutching a couple of CDs, Gopal was ready to rush out. "Maybe later Dad. I have to meet a friend."

For his son, burdened with his virgin mind, there were so many distractions. Divya gripped Sharma's arm. "Gopal wants to try a montage. The essence of an evening raga, then interpretation with jazz."

"Oh?"

He heard her whistle of exasperation. "I wish you'd asked him yourself." The hurt must have shown plainly on his face. Her eyes dilated as she looked up. He heard the softness in her voice. "Let's go into the study. I want to hear your new piece."

The pleats of her weekend silk sari rustled as she walked. A sudden tenderness washed over him. As she listened, he could feel her search for the special things he had talked about. It was true, he told himself, she heard his flute sing of impossible sounds. Moving clouds, shuddering stones, the opening of petals. Sounds of the soundless.

By the time he finished playing, it was dark outside. The last bittersweet note roamed the air in the room. From where Sharma stood, shadows of tiny leaves mottled her skin. He moved closer, saw that she was asleep. She traveled to Gopal, lips fanned out in a dream.

౼

Every Sunday, they went on a family outing downtown. This week, Divya wanted to see "Glimpses," a new exhibition at the Art Gallery of Ontario. She had seen the ad in the paper and shown it to Gopal. "What is it about?" Sharma asked in the car.

"Oh, it's very au courant," she said laughing. "Not easel and paint stuff."

Her tone had been flippant, she looked straight ahead without meeting his eyes. He knew this mood; if they were home she'd be listening to her favorite jazz station in a trance. "What do you see in that?" he blurted last time, "This is not in our blood." Personally, he would have preferred a trip to the Science Center. It would be educational for Gopal, for all of them.

The sculpture in the center was titled "Voulez-vous couchez avec moi?" It was the first line of an old rock song, Gopal explained. The artist had tossed layers of hay onto a camp cot. In the middle lay a slightly baked dough man. The tunnel mouth, hastily dug out, showed that he was dead. The viewers ahead became hushed. Sharma noticed a thick red thread curving down from the lipless mouth. "What is that?" he hissed into her ear, startling her with his tone. His face registered shock.

"The art of reality. Ketchup, I think," she said.

Scenic rectangles in blues and greens, faces carrying weighty abstractions, these he could understand. This art of reality, he knew nothing about that.

Gopal called out to them. "I like this one."

It was a castaway boat. Different lengths of nautical rope twisted into strange shapes were scattered inside. The boat was real, it had belonged to a fisherman in Greece, the placard said.

Then there were rows of photographs. Pictures of children that spoke of the lust of adults.

Finally, they walked past bits of discarded machinery, a chocolate sculpture of what looked like an octopus lifting weights. Sharma wanted coffee, he said he'd wait outside.

ᑫᗡ

A *jugalbandi* from the CD player in the bedroom—Chaurasia and Shiv Kumar Sharma performing an evening raga. Yawning, she picked up her book and turned to the story where she last left off. He noticed Divya had folded the top corner, scattered the pages with pencil ticks, grading paragraphs, as if the author cared what she thought. "You're doing that to a library book?" he said.

"So what. Stop peeking over my shoulder." A trace of flexing, lips beginning to pucker then falling back, amused with his self-righteousness. The music on the tape was gathering momentum. Closing his eyes, he listened to it for a few minutes before reaching out to the night table, picking up his own book.

She giggled and maneuvered chilly feet under legs. She did this often, sticking a frigid palm into his chest, pretending it was an endearing gesture, romantic somehow. Her long hair was flung back over the pillow. "What is it about?" he asked, shifting his position, freeing himself from the tangle of her legs.

She turned and looked him in the face. "About sex. Why don't you read it and find out?" His head throbbed as the music peaked; the wailing of the flute urgent, the tinkling sounds of the santoor violent in their leaping. Looking at Sharma, she laughed out loud. "Oh, don't be so serious. I'm just clowning around." Playing again, showing off. It was childish, this affinity with shock.

In the middle of the night, he reached out to her. His palm slapped empty space. He heard voices in the den downstairs, he could see a faint light. Divya sat on the sofa in her peach nightshirt, sipping from a glass. The television screen showed a couple in bed, the woman making animal sounds. Eyes pasted on the screen she sat, breasts heavy through the flimsy nightshirt, two ripe mangoes, ready to be plucked. He thought if he took one in his mouth, gums would blister from oozing sap. With one hand she clutched at her gut as if the man punched as he thrust. Sharma saw her areola and nipples poke through, dark knobs poised to alarm. He raised his hand then let it fall. Entranced by passion, she didn't see him there.

⟨∽⟩

Monday morning, Sharma stood looking at the view from the pier. Lake Ontario stretched out endlessly. It was no lake really. In this continent, even nature didn't know boundaries. The lake stretched out like a giant metal sheet, inscrutable, still and quiet. None of the endless churning, that noisy sea he observed in Madras. He thought of what Divya had said when they stood here last winter. She relished the white and muffled landscape of winter, the silence still and deep, the only sounds coming from your own head and heart.

He walked back towards the house on Rebecca Street.

In Reinhart's office, watching the eclipse on the news after class, he thought of Divya in front of the keyboard and screen under florescent lights. Gopal and his friends probably stared at the sky during recess with special glasses that protected eyes. In India, men stood knee-deep in water, mastering mantras that exorcised. Here, he was far from the crowd. Sharma saw thin streaks of the corona flaming at the edges, the center a dark hole, swallowed by the moon.

At the dinner table, "Did you see it?" he probed. Divya shrugged. Gopal cut in. His words were measured, there was only the slightest inflection in his voice when he spoke.

"Dad, what is the big deal? Imagine—scientists say there'll be a time with no sun at all." Divya put her fork down. "Mom, I got an A on my science project." Mother and son shared a half-smile. They talked about his fusion piece, the way it had evolved, an original raga braiding Indian music and jazz.

"Look. You've made your father speechless," she said, piling rice on Sharma's plate, winking at the same time. Then to Gopal she said, "Ask now."

"Dad, I've been practicing ragas on my own with Mom's help. Will you teach me on Sundays?"

Sharma stared at Divya, the way she surprised. All these years together and it was at that moment he noticed thread lines raveling across her forehead, the spreading border of the parting in the middle of her scalp. Why had he not seen this, her agility, spanning continents, skipping oceans?

Cool Wedding

DEAR LAKSHMI:

In the summer, this place is like India: Bombay, Madras, only fancy name—Houston, Pouston, America. My skin feels like bubble gum even after fresh oil bath. I am wearing eggplant color handloom sari, oiling and plaiting hair, putting kumkum tikka on forehead and going to puja room in closet. I am placing banana bunch and broken coconut on stainless steel thali before Ganesh, lighting four sandalwood incense sticks. Please God, remover of obstacles, I am saying, wake up my shakti part. You have placed me here in America. Help me influence husband Cheenu, children, Sudhir, Sushila and Siddharth. I am doing namaskaram prostration then crossing my hands, touching opposite earlobe, and squatting and standing, squatting and standing, physical penance before Ganesha. He is kindly forgiving all wrong tendencies on my part. This also helping my fitness program.

You know I always say we Indians not believing in psychologist, therapist, why talk to strangers when you can talk to close sister, after all, nothing like family, though spoiled children and husband make me question that wisdom sometimes. Did I know married life in America would turn out this way, that day when Cheenu came to our flat in Matunga, and I was only nineteen, rosebud faced in emerald Binny silk sari? Even after marriage, and Sudhir and Sushila coming along in New Jersey, then Siddharth belated surprise in Texas, I did not have any inkling of my present life.

Anyway, you asked about my job, my trip to Louisiana—our nephew Vikram's wedding; yes, cousin Leela was there with Dhakshisriramabadran, and I saw the Patels, Ila and Arun. I will try to tell you, bring you up-to-date on all those things including the difficulties in my family life. Since I returned from the wedding, too many things to attend to: children's academics, health problem, matching client difficulties. I tell you, often I wonder, what is the meaning of this modern life?

༄

Last Wednesday evening, I went to Sudhir's school meeting. You know hubby Cheenu is not going, always watching sports on TV. Coming home from work, then sitting with potato chips in front of TV. He is paying for ESPN, golf channel, God knows what else. You know I am not having time for TV, all rubbish they are showing anyhow. I am only watching news and i channel. International channel is showing nice Indian movies; you know I still like to watch Hindi movies, I don't like to forget language I learned in Bombay since childhood, this America and all, it is not reaching my blood.

You know Sudhir is in expensive private Episcopal school, very fancy that one. All mothers wearing such strong perfume, so crowded in chapel where we are meeting with college counselor, it is too much, I am sneezing too many times. You know Sudhir has to take SAT in a few months. I hope and pray he will do well. Lakshmi, you will not believe the competition in America. What with all the smart Chinese children. Thank God for the Americans. Without them, how will our children shine in America? I, personally, am very glad about the policy of one child only per couple in China. Wish the Chinese in America would also take it up.

Anyway, so I come home from the meeting and put on fan in the family room.

"Bring me some water," I am telling Sudhir, that boy. "All that perfume your school mothers are wearing, I am getting headache, bring also that Tylenol."

"I need the car, Ma," he is saying, "I have to visit Karen, group project for math. Everybody's meeting with their groups. Promise, I'll be careful with the car."

"Don't talk to me about car, buster, those two traffic tickets, who is going to pay for that?"

"No more tickets, I promise, please Mom, please."

I am telling that boy, "You better shape up after all this sleeping and sleeping in the summer. Your father and I are working like crazy, you better work like anything. Just wanting to do medicine is not enough. Nothing we want is going to fall from the sky." That cheeky fellow, your darling nephew as you call him, you know what he says?

"Who told you I want to do medicine, I'm thinking maybe law, history, dentistry. Am still undecided, Ma."

"This undecided not deciding and all is fancy American talk, you will make me old talking like that," I tell him."

Tell me Lakshmi, you think that Vimala Vaidyanathan's children, son-in-laws and daughter-in-law talked like him? She is displaying blown-up family photograph in her oversized den always saying pathologist, cardiologist, oncologist, neo-natologist, urologist, neurologist. Already there is one black sheep in our family, daughter Sushila, doing math. Don't get me started I tell you. All that praise from her teachers,

"Your girl's so bright Mrs Srinivasan." What is the use of that?

"Pure math is what I want to do Ma," Sushila said, and I replied,

"What are you, famous mathematician Ramanujam?"

Too much of this confidence-ponfidence, that is your niece's problem, Lakshmi, I am telling you. "He's so cute," she is saying this summer talking to her friend on the phone about some idiot classmate in UT Austin, thinking I am deaf in the next room. "So sue me, Ma," Sushila says, in that stylish way of hers, "I like him, so what?" I am thinking, am I a fool?

Why should I sue her when I can pinch her if I want? I am telling you, Lakshmi, mothering in America is so stressful. When I start to think of all that freedom in college, I cannot sleep sometimes. What is this cute-shoot rubbish showing off her figure wearing tight T-shirts all the time? It's not nice for a grown-up girl advertising everything like that. Really this Cheenu, your brother-in-law, should also be doing father's job. What is the use of only mother scolding children all the time? The way some of the other Indian parents are suffering, I am telling you, it is very worrying sometimes. Daughters and sons jumping over fence after lights are out, American dates waiting in Cherokee jeep cars, so many children lying, parents not knowing, no communication, very sad, this America, too much pressure to conform.

"What is the point?" I am asking Cheenu, "Talking about others, what are you doing to help me in this house Mister, never scolding children, making me the heavy (American talk), always working and watching sports, is that job of good father? Again he is smiling and pushing up his specs, I am getting mad and walking out. Anyway, sometimes I am getting so fed up, feel like being American myself saying none of my business, let them all fly a kite.

Yes, yes, don't worry, I'm getting to the wedding in Louisiana.

～∽～

I know it is more than three weeks since your letter came and I am writing back late, one section yesterday, another today. What with one thing and another thing. I am only wanting peace and quiet to be good matchmaker, sensitive mother and wife, you know I don't like to complain, that's not part of my style. But for peace and quiet, you need cooperation from family, husband and children, none is forthcoming from either direction, I can tell you that. Sometimes this matchmaking job I tell you, it is too much. But thank God. Since Cheenu helped me with my web page on the internet, my phone bills are not so fat. That is something at least. Tell me what you think of my new web site. Copied it down for you to read next. After all, if you cannot depend on close sister for advice, criticism, who can you turn to?

www. ShubhMangalam.SiteofAuspiciousMarriage

Say yes the Hindu Way : First comes marriage, then comes love:
Earthly bliss and Heavenly joy.

<u>Celebrating Whole Decade of Fruitful Matchmaking.</u>

When it comes to the needs of your family and friends,
Shoba Srinivasan is capable of attachment and detachment.
I take care to meet your subjective mate requirements on this end
while performing all potential spouse search tasks with objective
outlook on other end.

All cases accepted.
Caste / Nationality No Bar.
Single-Time Sincere Divorcees Okay.
We are not discriminating on basis of color, religion or mixed-marriage
results.

This is the Shubh Mangalam way, where list of potential spouse
is always qualitative and quantitative, in short—**fantastic.**
We cater to astrology / horoscope believers and modern non-believers.

Shubh Mangalam.SiteofAuspiciousMarriage
Say yes the Hindu Way.

Sugar Land, Houston, Texas, USA.
Cash (only) transactions arranged after first meeting.

Anyway, next month, matchmaking results will be good. Prospects
are promising, let me leave it at that. With Syrian Christian Malayali family in Chicago, I will hopefully be making four thousand after taxes, not
bad. Psychiatrist boy wanting demure wife, not job-taking type. "Enough

stress in my job for both of us," he said. What to do, I thought, difficult to find modern girls to agree to such demands. Luckily for me, I met grandmother visiting from Trivandrum at Onam festival lunch in big Woodlands house. Very grand affair with real rose kolam design at the entrance, so many fancy cars: Mercedes, Acura, BMW and all, they are asking us Toyotas to park very far from the house. "Patience," I am telling Cheenu also, "Enda, you know my matchmaking job, I need these people, what to do, such is life."

"C'est la vie," as our sister is saying in Louisiana during the wedding, I am coming to that, wait.

Really Lakshmi, why all this materialism? Very sickening, this attitude. Woodlands house for Onam lunch has big swimming pool like lima bean. Everybody standing around, no place to move, so I am bumping into elbow of Trivandrum grandmother with demure granddaughter, loving States, watching *Dallas* on TV, crazy about Texas, only twenty, finishing senior year at Loretto House in Calcutta, very easy going, fair, slim, smiling type. Now only remaining problem is matching horoscopes and you know that is not in our hands, God will do the rest. I am going regularly to the temple you know we have Meenakshi temple in Houston, very beautiful and nice.

☙

This squeezing in motherhood, wifehood into my demanding job, it's very obstructive sometimes. And on top of that, like a fool, I tried to make the children and Cheenu puri, korma, fresh rice for yogurt rice and condensed milk payasam for dessert because it was Friday. You know I make a point of the family observing some prayer time and proper South Indian meal at least one auspicious evening a week. Keeping in touch with our culture is so important I tell you, I am seeing so many who are lost.

I am hurrying up, finished grinding the coffee beans for dikakshun extract, Saturday night before going to bed. Sudhir and Sushila being teenagers do not get up till ten o'clock on Sunday morning. If we slept late when we were growing up in Bombay, Amma scolded and Appa turned off the Bajaj fan and dragged the pillow from under our heads. India built character muscle. Not that we need to brag. A little discipline, some suffering, it's good for the soul, no? Otherwise, how do these children grow depth? Too much cushioning and softness, all this choice in America, it's not very good. Anyway, what is done is done, I married Cheenu and now we are here not there. Not that I'm complaining. Still.

Your dear brother-in-law Cheenu can enforce some discipline, give them deadline for waking up, not encouraging bad behavior, you know this is how problems start. "Who knows where it will lead?" I tell him, giving him coffee in nice stainless steel tumbler. He is nodding as if serious and pushing his specs back to the top of his nose, whistling all the way to the den. By the time I finish my bowl of Golden Grahams, (you know my weakness, I am loving American sweet cereals) I hear him laughing and watching Simpsons with Sudhir, Sushila and Siddharth.

At last children are in their rooms—Sudhir on the phone telling me homework, Sushila washing hair using enough water for whole family in India, Siddharth my innocent baby, really doing homework, having slight problem with fractions, never mind.

Anyway, Cheenu and I are both relaxing for few minutes. I am telling him also, "What are you doing? What is the meaning of working all week and watching news and sports on TV every weekend? Same same all the time. Do something new with your time. Always the same business it's not nice."

On Friday afternoons, he is going with friends for golf, talking about playing sports, sitting and driving around course in cart, then nicely lying to me, saying, "working out . . ." On top of that, he is drinking beer with friends, saying, "Why not enjoy only?" when he comes home and I ask. Then he is thinking he can make up by trying to kiss me. But you know how your brother-in-law is. He thinks he knows everything, only office business and golf, tennis scores swimming in his head all the time. Life is also about other things, no? I am telling him "arré baba, do some sit-ups some exercise, this golf-polf once a week, it is not enough."

"I know about you," I tell him, "your type A personality, look at your Ganesh tummy like big coconut, work, work, all the time, lifting your company on your head, Fluor Daniel this and Fluor Daniel that. I am not Mrs Daniel, remember that. There are three children to be educated in this family, buster, I can't do it alone. I want you healthy so you can live a long time. What is the point of being married becoming widow stuck with children all the time?"

Only yesterday, before my bath, I am looking at myself in the full length mirror and thinking, not bad, talking to myself. Forty-two years old and still curvy-purvy, like slightly plump Janaki from Chingelpet. Now you better get serious, I am thinking, in this family, if you don't get serious, then who will? Then your brother-in-law Cheenu is coming in, whistling at me like I am some blonde on TV ad. "Arré," I am saying, "What is all this middle-aged lust? I am not your Monica-Ponica sitting in some White House. This is Shoba Srinivasan from Matunga, remember that."

Yes, about the wedding in Louisiana, I am coming to that soon.

సొ

I am going to the kitchen, cutting brinjal and onion for sambhar, finished frying mustard, then comes Siddharth, saying, "Call me Sid."

"Arré," I am saying, "why I am bothering suffering with you big, American, super-size son, cesarean section, labour for hours and hours, coming out saying, ' "Don't call me Siddharth Ma, my name is Sid." ' What is this dirty habit, nice Indian name Siddharth—this Sid-Pid—chopping your name so rudely like that?"

He is saying, "What's this brown stuff, Ma? Sambhar? Not again. I like fried chicken, Kentucky, man."

"I don't do this chicken business," I tell him, "Eating birds and such. You want smart brains, eat fried bhindi, okra, we ate that for good grades in math. You become back-talking like your big brother and sister, I will pinch your buttocks, buster junior, remember that."

In the middle of all this commotion, you know I have to help prepare for the wedding in Baton Rouge. That dear sister of ours, Padma, very stylish and sophisticated, I don't want to gossip and complain all the time, you know I don't like to do that, but she is calling me ten times a day, saying, "What do I do about this and what do I do about that?" Arré, what is the use of post-graduate degree in psychology and women's studies, cannot help organize son's wedding? Why all this botheration when Cajun bride's Robichaud family in Denham Springs, Louisiana, offering house, having only pool wedding, fifty people, saying they don't believe in anything grand?

Anyway, so I am calling bride's mother for names of Cajun dishes, then phoning catering people, ordering: palak paneer, pulao, dhal, chicken curry, gumbo, jambalaya, crawfish éttoufée, this strange combination, you better set up separate vegetarian and non-vegetarian tables, why did you invite cousin Leela and family from Calgary, Alberta, they are coming with purist Hindu food notions and all?

Then she is saying, "Never mind about that, I am worried about Cajun granny from gulf coast, she wants rehearsal dinner, supposed to be given by groom's family. Did Esther's mother talk to you about that?"

"No," I am saying, now worrying along with Padma. I am telling you Lakshmi, Cajun granny is behaving like Pope's right foot. What is the use of Catholic-matholic tradition? Granddaughter not even wearing white dress, choosing pistachio gown from Dillard's. Bride Esther and groom Vikram-Bakram having it off months before the wedding living in same apartment. These children today, no respect for marriage, holy institution should be approached with respect. Even those of us approaching with respect getting problems back. Those two should be ashamed, none of my business, I tell you, you know I don't like to interfere, let them do what they like.

⌒

So I drive down for a week to Baton Rouge leaving Cheenu, children, and clients, since Padma calling and pleading too many times. She does not know what to serve for rehearsal dinner, menu planning and cooking, she cannot do that. Anyway, so I go into her kitchen and think, good that I'm adjustable, eating eggs, and cheese, and baked goods because her fridge is full of brown, organic, oval eggs laid by chicken that run wild not caged in pens.

"Padma," I am saying to our dear sister, "This eating scrambled eggs, toast, salad, soup, all the time—no wonder you cannot think, nervous about small thing like cooking. Get some dhal, chapati, rice in your life." But she is not listening to my sensible words, inviting me to join her awareness workshop in massage therapist's office same evening.

Anyway, so two days before rehearsal dinner I go with our sister to awareness workshop in borrowed massage therapist's office. Very crowded with office furniture, tables in the middle, chairs pushed against the wall. All the women wearing black leotards. Me in my purple sari with yellow border, you know I still wear only Indian clothes, this is best in humid climate, airy feeling, breeze flowing in and out. Padma's assistant friend is putting on new-age music, strange hollow tube noises, everybody starting out, inviting wild Kali woman inside to come out. Wriggling like caterpillar black bodies on the floor, then rising, opening pieces of netted fabric from Michael's, (famous American craft shop) cloth wings stretching into butterflies. Women dancing all over the place, around massage therapist's table, I get knee cramps pretending like the rest. For the remainder of hollow tube song, I am standing near filing cabinet in the kitchen which is so narrow my throbbing knee is jutting out.

"This goddess-poddess game, wild woman thing, is not for somebody like me," I am telling everybody.

They are saying, "Let it out, push the anger out." What is the use of so many angry women in black leotards playing caterpillar-butterfly? Metamorphosis should be happening in your head, not happening from dancing around office furniture. I too am angry but smart enough to know that. Anyway, none of my business I tell you, this awareness-she-wareness, strange modern invention, did Cajun granny become demanding granny doing butterfly dance?

I am calling Cheenu daily, telling that Sudhir to work hard, that Sushila she is by nature hardworking, only has this eye for the boys. I am telling her also, "focus on studies, that is your job." And my baby Siddharth, you know he is the innocent type, only interested in food, chicken, chicken, nothing else.

On day of rehearsal dinner, Cheenu is calling me from cell phone, Sushila late coming from Austin, they are leaving soon, on their way in no time. Next phone call is collect from Leela they are also arriving soon, plane late leaving from Calgary, you know that Canada, all that Quebecois French Canadian nonsense, efficiency going down toilet, what to do, such is life. Anyway, four hours later, cousin Leela and husband are walking into the house. She has not changed a bit, I tell you, wearing heavy jewelry like Christmas tree, so much ornamentation is not nice.

At rehearsal dinner, you know I made my specialties: pulao, korma, kofta curry, puris, idli, chutney. Everything came out very nice. Leela is talking loudly like always. Joking and laughing with Cajun granny, who does not seem so tough, liking my cooking, after all. Our dear co-brother-in-law, Leela's husband Dhakshisriramabadran, wearing pretty red velvet bowtie, sitting quiet like meditating mouse, while our dear cousin talking and laughing with everybody, again and again, all that jewelry shaking, no moderation, decorum, always bumptious, that one.

The Cajuns cannot pronounce our beautiful Indian names. Americans cannot say Dhakshisriramabadran Velayathur Venkatraman or any long name like that. Same problem all Indians are having, talking on the phone, giving our name for reservation or anything like that. If American at other end, typing name on keyboard, south Indian speaking, spelling out the letters, saying, D as in Donkey A as in America and so on till the end of the name and American on other end saying computer screen space not enough, name too difficult, long, which country is that from? Anyway, so poor co-brother-in-law Dhakshisriramabadran, trying to be adjustable, telling bride's father, "Mr Robichaud, call me Dhakshi." But all Robichauds and Boudreaux men already giddy from Budweiser beer, saying together,

"Say what, bubba, Ducksheet?"

And all children and teenagers within hearing distance laughing including my own Sudhir, Sushila, Siddharth. I tell you, these children today, no respect for adults.

Anyway, rehearsal dinner is big success. We are finishing off with lad-
dus, pedas and gulab jamuns from Bombay Sweets in Houston. "Sweets
and all," I told our dear sister, "better order only, I cannot do that."

Thank God, after rehearsal dinner, Cheenu and I are getting one day
rest. Everybody else going to Nottoway plantation, and Padma's organic
picnic lunch. Only hubby and I are not going.

We are getting invitation from Cheenu's old office friend, Patel, you
know Ila and Arun from when you lived in Toronto. He used to be with
Fluor, now with Exxon. They live here in Baton Rouge, owning chain
of motels on Florida Boulevard. That Ila and Arun, too forward I tell
you, having love marriage twenty-seven years ago, now throwing big
party for anniversary. You remember from before, they have one
showoffy son, always wearing cellular phone, beeper, whole Radio Shack
store on his belt. Twenty-four years old, already earning six-figure salary
in motel business. What is the meaning of money? No value these days,
I can tell you that. Anyway, so Cheenu is showing me invitation from
Patels, big pink carnation flower on left side, glitter powder stuck on the
petals, dew drops on the leaves and Hinglish words on the right. You
know these Gujeratis, thinking in Hindi-Gujerati, writing in English,
always mixing Indian English and American English, they cannot talk
good English like us south Indians to save their life. Anyway, I copied
the words for you. I know you like to hear everything, leave nothing out,
you always say, I am giving details like you want.

ANNIVERSARY PARTY INVITATION

Before our happy, auspicious marriage, people said we were an
UNLIKELY AND UNMATCHED PAIR
Some said PERSONALITY-wise difference,
Others said NATURE-wise difference
Elders said HOROSCOPE-wise incompatibility,
Neighbors and friends said OTHER-wise unseen difficulty

HEY, Y'All: WE ARE STILL JOYOUSLY MARRIED
TO THE SAME PERSON EACH OF US

Merry times await you at
Plantation Banquet Hall
Quality Inn, February 8, 7:00 PM

No gifts please. Your presence will be our present.

Ila and Arun Patel
4656 Inverness Drive,
CCLA: Country Club of Louisiana (housing golf course designed
by many times winner of emerald jacket Golden Bear Jack
Nicklaus
Baton Rouge, LA 70808

At the party, Ila is the same like always, talking with lipstick on her teeth. "You know my beta, son Suresh (whole Radio Shack store on his belt, I am adding) went to Bombay to brush up Gujerati, seek prospective bride. So far, nothing worked out," she said, licking her teeth, swallowing her lipstick and holding my hand. "Poor fellow," she said, "landing in Bombay during monsoon rains so much water, car stalling, people pushing taxi, shouting dhakka marro, water over knee caps, nothing changes back home, only girls becoming too westernized, they used to be so reserved and homely types."

Then Arun, her husband, joining us and boasting to me, "The men in this family, we are always very peripatetic. Only Ila, she is homely type, does not like to deal with jet lag. Everybody in Indian community saying to her, you have everything, only waiting for daughter-in-law. So Mrs Shoba, I am requesting you to look for suitable girl. Keep an eye out. No rush. After all, my beta, you know he is only twenty-four. We want girl with topnotch character. Only thing, you know our lifestyle, girl must be sociable, know how to talk with people, smile, and be without stress. You know we men already have too much of that. We want women with calming effect. Must be cultured. You know Ila is culture vulture type."

Outside I am saying all right, we will see what we can do. But inside I am thinking, why they want to take some too-young girl, mould her into this foolish wife? Before finding answer for my own question, I see Radio Shack boy coming near me, wearing big smile. He is having good manners, politeness I see, bringing me juice and saying namaste. He is asking, "How are you Auntie?" and offering plate of masala cashew nuts. Ila and Arun are leaving to greet new arriving guests. Radio Shack boy turns off on buttons of communication gadgets hanging from his belt and pocket: click click click and red glowing buttons turning black. He is bending his head low American style and talking to me softly.

"I hear that your business is doing well Auntie; all my friends are saying so. You are listening closely to the parents but not too much. They are saying you understand very well young people's views. That is very modern and good, Auntie, I like that." Then he is smiling and winking at me that foolish, charming boy. "You know I like mature and bold professional type," he is whispering. "Not this teeny bopper business desi Indian style."

༄

On the day of our dear nephew Vikram's wedding, bride is appearing in pistachio color gown, looking very nice. Good girl, that one, only has to learn our Indian ways. Not looking decent, sitting on Vikram's lap at breakfast time. Why these children today, wanting to do everything in front of everybody? All this flaunting is not nice. Anyway, that civil judge-priest, in black suit, very punctual, coming on dot of eleven, and all of us standing around pool, bride and groom exchanging vows, reading poetry, both looking into each other's eyes. Robichaud women crying, bringing Kleenexes out, and me praying, our dear nephew and his wife, dear Brahma, Siva, Narayana, let them stay together always, no divorce American style, that is all we simple people want.

After the wedding, reception is in backyard. Behind the big azalea bushes Robichaud and Boudreaux men arranging barrels of beer with tube spout coming out. I am standing near cake table, so many fern leaves stapled to lace cloth, flowers here and there, champagne glasses wearing ribbons, very beautiful and nice. Then I see Sushila with bride's brother Claude, English major at LSU. Cajun granny said he is writing love poetry Esther and Vikram exchanged to each other. You know English major type, long hair, black clothes even in Louisiana heat, smoking cigarette, dirty habit. I am watching very carefully, walking from cake table. Claude is pushing away strands of Sushila's hair, they are pretending to be Sonny and Cher, I can see that. I am staring at her very hard shaking my head no, all this is not nice. Then that Claude has seen me too, I can tell Sushila is mad by the way she is walking off. She will be complaining about me to him but that is okay, I say quite all right. I am only doing mother's job.

That husband Cheenu is nowhere to be found.

I find out Sudhir is in front of Acadian porch of Robichaud house, parking cars with other boys. Padma is calling me, something about Siddharth. I want to tell Sudhir, "No, not good idea. I don't know what kind of insurance policy those people have." You know he brought home two traffic tickets since summer. That brother-in-law of yours, Cheenu, he should be talking to Sudhir, doing father's job.

My baby Siddharth is in the kitchen complaining of tummy ache. He has eaten shrimp, he is saying. "How much?" I am asking.

"I don't know—maybe forty—something like that," he is saying.

"All that oily dip. Why this behavior, am I not feeding you?" I ask. I am taking him upstairs, saying, "Lie down. Maybe go to bathroom. Where is your father?" That Cheenu, you know he is always carrying Rolaids to neutralize Fluor job? Really these children, troubling like babies in middle of family occasion. I am giving Siddharth Maalox from Robichaud medicine cabinet, taking him to spare bedroom saying, "Lie down."

When I am opening the door, I hear the TV and who is there but your dear brother-in-law, Cheenu, no wonder I could not find him anywhere downstairs. He is watching TV, golf, I can see, smiling foolish smile. "Shoba, baby, it's PGA Finals. Don't be that way." I see reason for baby, foolish smile. Empty beer can near the chair, he is holding second can. I am always worrying about children, what is next problem, what are they going to do now? And he is drinking beer, enjoying life.

After lunch, catering big success, Sudhir and Sushila, all teenagers and American adults, dancing to music inside the house. Then Leela going in and joining. That silly Padma encouraging her. You know those two women in our family, never knowing limits, always getting carried away. Again poor Dhakshisriramabadran, standing and smiling and watching cousin Leela, teenagers, many adults doing Macarena. You know this is a fad now, latest American dance. Cajun granny also joining in. Everybody shaking bottom and slapping thighs, and sweating, really, this Leela must be knowing middle-aged Indian women do not have hips and figure to dance Macarena in public. Leela is looking like chapati dough shaking in earthquake. Chee! chee! like we used to say in India as children, shame shame poppy shame. Dhakshisriramabadran now sitting in corner again like meditating mouse.

Anyway, between you and me, hubby Cheenu is not totally zero father, he is telling Sudhir that boy in car driving back to Houston, "Be practical, career choice and all is okay but remember you have to look after yourself." Hubby also telling Sushila that girl, "Everybody having lust like Jimmy Carter. That is quite all right. Only hide this from public view, you know our Hindu community, pretending sex is okay on rocks, temple sculpture and all but not for people made of flesh and blood." And to baby Siddharth he is saying, "It does not matter if you are not clever at math. What is the use of being engineer working your balls off?" You know ditchwater language is very cool in America, what to do Lakshmi, cool becoming worldwide disease nobody wants inoculation for that one even I am doing fusion Bharath Natyam dirty dancing in shower. Those three children listening or not listening to hubby Cheenu, I don't know, only God knows. Anyway, for one minute, I am thinking not bad, I married smart man.

და

"Too bad you missed Vikram Krishnamoorthy and Esther Robichaud's cool wedding," Sudhir says to tell you. He says you would have loved that. I am not saying anything. You decide for yourself. You know my nature. I am not gossiping like the rest. We are family, after all, if you let down own family what is left in this modern life?

Anyway, after cool wedding, we are coming home exhausted and I have frozen dhal thawing in microwave, fresh rice from pressure cooker and papad. We are all happy to be home even the children though they don't admit anything. Going out and all is nice but nothing like coming to our own place, I tell you, I need same pillow, bed, even different bathroom is giving me problems, that Padma's organic sandwich, stomach-making noise all the time. Good to eat rice, have oil bath and rest my head on my own pillow, nothing like that I tell you. But when I am lying down after dinner, my mind still vibrating like pambaram, wooden top, must be all the excitement from cool wedding, I cannot fall asleep, my eyes are open like bird wings in the sky. So pretty soon I am counting baby elephants, praying and talking to Ganesha about job and family.

Anyway, between you and me, hubby Cheenu always laughing and understanding all my jokes. What is more important than that? Good sense of humor, that smart man. You know America, very optimistic country, people are always saying, Shoba, you are only forty-something years young so I am also thinking for some things, when in America do as the Americans do, keep trying to change hubby never give up men are like bread, be patient, give them time to rise.

So in the dark, I am turning to Cheenu, and saying, "What is all this mister? Sleeping sleeping night after night always the same thing it's not nice. What is all this Hingis-Pingis only watching tennis and golf why not care a little about wife, family? Only sports, office, sports, office, so American, that is not our style. Let us do something different. Why not imagine oval office, round office, I am getting feeling like playing White House."

Yours in affection and devotion,
Shoba

Third Eye

WHEN ANITA WAS BORN, I thought that nothing that happened before was of any importance. In the beginning, things had been simple. I would run to other mothers, join their talk about colic and gripe water. We swapped stories about sleeplessness and fatigue, we exchanged the latest books on post-natal care. For all of us Indian mothers in America, when daughters were little, posturing was fine. As the years passed and Anita grew up, I knew I had to prepare. With high school, the difference became official. Ajit, my husband, concurred with our friends. If we let Anita date, bigger things would follow. "Why don't you talk to her, explain how we feel?" he said. How blindly I had danced into this darkness called motherhood as if all there was to conquer was the physical side. Listening to him, moments like these, I felt I was leading somebody else's life.

It was an auspicious day, a day to honor the Goddess Lakshmi. When I asked Anita for help with the halva, the Eucharist that was offered during prayer, I thought it was a good time to bring it up. Perhaps I could help her understand. At least she wasn't like some of the others, sneaking around, lying to their parents. I had always thought of myself as an honest, up front sort of mother, I tried to talk to her about things. Three years ago, I had brought her a book called *Every Girl*. The blurb on the jacket said: "A clear, factual and sympathetic introduction to menstruation that will answer questions and meet emotional needs." When I was a girl, my mother hadn't said a thing. I had pieced it together from years of observation. On certain days of the month, the women in my family became polluted somehow. Sequestered by themselves, they couldn't touch the rest of us. They weren't allowed in the kitchen and the prayer room, they ate by themselves.

∽

I sat at the kitchen table, blanching almonds and humming along with the CD player. The glowing red lines of the spectrum analyzer danced to the sound of Carnatic music. Anita walked in holding a magazine. She was reading a review of *Monsoon Wedding*. Talking about Meera Nair, the director of the movie, Ajit had said in a plangent voice, "What does she know about Indian culture? She comes from Africa, she's married to a black man. She is in no position to judge." Sometimes when we watched TV and the camera zoomed in on a kiss, Ajit got up for water blocking the faces on the screen. Anita protested loudly, mourning the loss of the moment. Since she began to bloom, I noticed Ajit stooped slightly. It was as if he wanted to put a leash on time. For me, looking at her, watching her, I welled up inside.

"Anita, peel these cardamom pods," I said.

"Mom, do you mind?" She raised her eyebrows and shifted the selector to radio, locating her station.

I dipped my fingers into a big stainless steel bowl and said, "Who was that on the phone, a friend?" She stopped peeling to glance worriedly at her polished fingernails.

"Just Brian. He asked if I'd like to go to a movie Friday night. I said maybe. If I finish my paper on Willa Cather." I fished around the caramel colored water for nuts, pinching the ovals at the tip, the way my mother had taught me, forcing them to shed their skin. I dropped the naked nuts in a smaller bowl and wiped my hands with a towel. It was important that a mother be clear when talking about such things.

"Your father and I can take you to the movie," I blurted. There were stray droplets of water on the table. I cleaned up as I went along, nervous of a mess. Holding the black mustard-like seeds in one palm, Anita dragged the marble mortar and pestle closer to her.

"It's not the same," she sighed. "I want to go with him. To talk. He's really nice Mom." I stared into the bowl. Anita would be sulking now, flashing those Please Mom eyes.

"Nice," I mimicked. "What do you know about boys to tell who's nice?"

"You never let me go anywhere. Do anything. I'm almost sixteen." Anita crushed the seeds noisily, her elbow jutting out, moving up and down violently.

"That's the problem. You're only sixteen. What do you know about love, marriage, life?" I said.

Anita got up and gestured with her hands. "Love? Marriage? Life? What are you saying?" She spoke through clenched teeth, jaw rigid with control. I knew it was no time to hold back. Ajit's style was clean. I would have come along later, hovered around Anita's room.

"Not now Anita. Maybe later. When you're ready. You'll meet some nice Indian boy, get engaged, and then go out."

A couple of years ago, Anita had come home saying why did we have to be Indian, she was dying of embarrassment. The Social Studies book had pictures of frescoes from Ajanta and Ellora, showing big bosomy women, without any clothes. Her classmates had all looked at her and laughed. I got up slowly and adjusted the folds of my sari. She watched as I dropped the nuts into the blender and poured in some milk. I stabbed the mixture with a spatula to let the air out. While I fumbled for the switch, Anita pulled the plug and shouted in my face. "What? I'm an American, Mom. You think I want my life mapped out?" She held the waistband of her Levi's with her thumbs, her fists balled up tight. I slapped my forehead and shook my head.

"Think. Anita. We're not like them. Love, marriage—it isn't something you toss about."

"I know. Like you and Daddy." Anita's voice was brambly, high

70

pitched, she emphasized every word as if she were on stage. "Watching TV on your anniversary. That's love?" She began pacing back and forth like her father swallowing the kitchen with large, manly strides.

"Their love is not our kind of love," I pleaded. "Love comes after marriage. It's safe and strong. We're not fickle. We don't jump in and out of love. That's why we don't date." I watched my daughter's stiff back. Anita pressed her palms to her ears screeching:

"I don't want to hear it. I don't want to hear it." She ran out of the kitchen and kicked her bedroom door shut. I felt drained. Clean scuff marks, I wrote on the kitchen pad. As I held the blender lid down tight, I felt the throbbing underneath. This time, the familiar sound gave no comfort. I scooped the white puree into a heavy metal wok, the one I had carried all the way from Madras. Cushioned in my suitcase with saris, tucked in with rolled-up blouses along the sides, it had arrived snug and secure, not a single sign of damage.

The halva simmered gently under my constant attention. It had to be stirred relentlessly, coaxed to readiness, before it gave out a sweet, ripe smell. I remembered how my parents had fed me stories of demons that lurked in the world outside. I saw the halva come together, a single yielding mass, matching the picture in my mind. Rebellion, that easy, childish thing, was for the short-sighted. I poured the halva carefully into a greased mold, smoothed the surface and left it to cool.

I thought about what Anita had said. About me and Ajit. He worked hard as a hospital administrator. As for going places, did I need frills like that? I took pleasure in doing little things. When he bunched up his towel after a shower, I straightened it out. In the prayer room, I made sure the lamp was lit. At night, Ajit bolted and locked the doors; I inspected for dripping taps. Maybe tonight, when we were in bed, I would ask. I would turn to him and say: "Do you love me that way? Do you think I'm pretty?" Such a silly question. He might laugh.

The halva had cooled. When I traded recipes, I noticed that others called it halva while it was still pasty. I understood that they worried about economy. But I agreed with Ajit. This was America, you needn't grip your wallet so hard. With the knife in my hand, I carved diagonal lines. Then I counted the pieces and used the fleshy inside of my thumb to glide in an almond, an imprint in the heart of each diamond. It added a little decorative touch.

ᗡ

Anita was rummaging through my bathroom cabinets. She spotted me at the doorway and spoke in a raspy, sullen tone: "I need a tampon. I've got my period." Her eyes scanned a gaping bottom drawer. I was in the bathroom now, extracting a box from behind a pile of bath towels.

"Here," I offered, a gesture of reconciliation. Anita grabbed the box from me, her fingers brushing mine. My left eye twitched. Anita had forgotten what this meant. Touching me, helping with the halva, she'd contaminated it all.

In the prayer room, I placed the statue of the goddess on a wooden slab. She carried a citron, a shield and drinking vessel. On her head sat a coiled snake. Her face shone with a golden pallor matching the glow of her elaborate ornaments. That vague trace of a smile bored into my heart as if she was about to relay some special message. When the Gods couldn't destroy their demons, they had turned to Lakshmi. Coming to the battlefield alone, she had used her delicate body, her gentle words and sidelong glances to befuddle her enemies, an enigma till the end. Was she Parvati, the beautiful, passionate woman or Kali, the horrific and bloodthirsty side strewing death and destruction? What cunning men have, to weave myths and stories, to put woman on a pedestal, removed from life. This was the ultimate maya then, a convenient illusion.

ᗡ

Anita walked in, cupping flowers in her palms. I carried in auspicious powders—yellow turmeric for intellect and vermilion for love. I placed a tray with a container of halva, fruits and grains before the Goddess.

We began drawing kolams on the floor, labyrinth designs with rice flour. I remembered watching my mother drawing patterns outside the threshold of our house in Madras. She had fed myriads of ants every day, ensuring they stayed outside. Men had their mantras, women their

72

quiet language of symbols.

I took a pinch of the vermilion and pressed it to Anita's forehead.

"A dot represents the divine eye, the Goddess within you," I said. Anita stared back, a blank expression on her face. "The dot is a continuous line that stands for the unbroken, perfect whole," I explained. She threw a piercing look as I held a small mirror to my face and brought my fingers to my own forehead.

When I was little, store-bought collyrium had been the rage. My mother had used a safety pin head to paint the forehead with a glistening fish eye. Fashion moved in circles. Grandmother's vermilion powder became a sticker book; self-adhesive felt circles filled pages in lively red. Spheres blurred. Upturned teardrops took their place. Then shapes like stars and clovers stuck to the face.

Later that night, I walked into Anita's room.

"About the movie you want to see. I've decided to let you go. Don't say anything about this to your father. Do you understand?"

༄

The garage door groaned and yawned before Ajit walked in, late as usual, tired from yet another week of juggling numbers. Seeing the silent TV screen, he turned to me. "Where's Anita?"

"At Anjali's house. Some group project." I flipped through the pages of *Seventeen* stopping at an illustration. The artist had dabbed aubergine on the skirt; tufts of woolen threads wiggled to life.

"Who's Anjali?" he probed, squinting at the short kilts, willowy thighs and legs sticking out.

"Don't you remember? The new Sri Lankan family who moved here last month." It had come out so easily. Impressed by my own audacity, I quickly sealed the lie. "I have to pick her up at nine-thirty." We had arranged for Anita to wait at McDonald's on the main road. Ajit shuffled towards the corridor leading to our bedroom. Satisfied of her safety, he lost interest. Sri Lankan was close enough. The Asian cocoon swelled when you lived in America. I watched him from the back, toppling his columns, all debits and credits neatly organized. Staring at my daughter's first photograph on the wall—that tiny, crumpled face—I thought—so now you and I, we are inextricably linked. I clutched the moment stretching the thrill like a child.

When I picked her up, there were the signs: the animated gestures, the breathless speech, the half pronouncements. She might think I couldn't understand. Would she think that I'd admonish her for this opulence? I said nothing. She must think that this is solely hers.

Attar

WHEN RAJAS SAT IN PALACES, necks tilted with gems; streets were strewn with mosques, temples, artisans; merchants everywhere; holy men bundled under trees; a young woman whispered to another a tale the shape of curved talons. "An enigma," she said, "a magical scent from a flower, hushed yearning that possessed." In villages and towns, people shared rituals, smearing rashes with the sap of herbs, stewing aromatic gums and balsams, tucking petals into hair, bosoms, men sealing pores with sandalwood. And in all the homes, walls patted with cow dung, lime washed or lined with art, oblations of incense to Gods, perfumes transcending the world, cavorting with the spirits. This was an era of wonder, economics; emeralds, pepper and patchouli luring traders from distant lands.

Twilight to moonlight, in the town of Mayapur, not far from Surat, the ankle-bells of Begum Shahida, fourth wife of the nawab of Zarba, echoed around rose roots in the garden. Eunuchs with their betel stained lips and snake amulets spoke of the Begum with topaz eyes. Shahida, they said, had discovered a perfume so pure, so potent, that madness of some kind tempted the woman to risk it all.

The nawab, dallying by the window with his second wife, saw

Shahida's fingers brush Paul Glasgow's palm. Full of suspicions and noble wisdom, he banished the cursed woman out of sight. He referred to the great Ibn-Sina of Persia. Didn't he assess temperament of the brain from the color of the eyes? Tiger eyes so fickle, now gold, now brown.

Since her disappearance, Shahida's story, told and retold by many, was stitched from bits of this and that. They said that she had been spotted at a stall in the bazaar, that she had moved on to another passion—jasmine, that dramatic and contradictory flower. There was talk of the fountain in the garden where she had spent most of her time. Coming from the women's quarters, eunuch harem guards gesticulated wildly, sweeping arms showing jets of water, the scent of oil residue that rose from the pond. Hushed voices spoke of birds that dove in and out, spreading wings, perfuming air. Shahida's recipe for wayward lovers continued to circulate among girls and wives. To add to the confusion, there were whispers of her spirit hovering over the sea which some said had swallowed her up.

❧

She was the daughter of an herbalist, father unknown to all but the mother. The small house of her childhood was occupied by an assortment of temple and nautch dancers, riddle tellers, psychics who entered the future with talking birds and diagrams. A strangely stubborn and sickly child, she grew quickly, resistant enough to survive. At the age of eight, there were pox bubbles following the fever, popping and sizzling on the tongue, rushing into caves of tonsils. Her skin tingled madly, the anus peeled and swelled, bumps of onion skin. Mother brushed a muslin *punkah* along her forehead, silk tassels on creases behind knees, cotton balls between ridges on bald underarms. Shahida squirmed and rubbed a single ear against the sheets. Where the other ear should have been was a misshapen bit of flesh, a ball of dough, blemishless.

Mother entered their room upstairs late in the morning, bringing festoons of leaves to hang from doors dividing the house. Smelling like moss, the woman lifted the patient's palms and clucked at sharp fingernails. Peeling away layers of clothes, she played connect the dots, painting the skin with a bitter concoction of tender ferns, margosa leaves. "What is that for?" Mossy mother scolded and shushed.

"To make you well, now sleep in peace." Mother gave daughter a rose to eat. The tang of petals on the tongue numbed the burning on her skin. A warm breeze entered the house and ran through the rooms. Grabbing the pestilence that clung to the walls, it made the leaves rise and fall. Watching greenness swell and roll, Shahida fell asleep.

By the time she was twelve, she discovered ways to release mucus pearls that crowded sinus pockets, pat sheaths of poultice from plant pulp. She watched intently when dogs played cow and devoured grass, thumbing through books, discovering the power of oils, scented barks and resins, strategies for aromatic healing, shamans and alchemists flying from ear to non-ear.

Behind the rope swing in the garden, she discovered a strange plant. Averse to touch when seed vessels were ripe, the petals reacted by separating, curling, spitting seeds out of the base of the cup. The slightest threat of contact, a hem line rushing past, the vibration of a proferred finger, and the plant performed. She taught others in the house to pinch and sniff sweet basil when tired; crushed and patted the paste of castor oil plants on cracked heels of dancing women. While other girls drew henna paisleys over clammy palms, headlines and lifelines, she strained the essence of a hundred flowers, throwing netted cloth with the washing, enticing bees and wasps.

When mother made her rounds through the town, Shahida observed patients, restless for her own. "You must learn to wait," mother warned. To teach herself patience, she got a mynah from the bazaar. She hung the cage on the tip of a branch outside her window so the bird was still part of the world outside. Every morning, she read verses out loud without glancing in his direction, repeating the words carefully, over and over again, till she didn't need the book, her girlish voice rising from the bed, turning pages from the book in her mind. Then Shahida got up to shut the window which she opened again at night. After ten months, when she slipped into the garden on a new-moon night, she heard the bird trill the words, standing on one leg.

The first time Shahida smelled a rose, she walked in a trance, mind sliding down petals, pollen grit on the tongue. Avoiding the serrated leaves and thorns, she picked up the severed head of an old flower. She drank in the scent greedily, the fragrance carrying her out of herself.

The value of scent, mother said, is known by all. See them bring flowers to the grave, float petals with ashes on the river. Watch how the women ornament their bodies before meeting their men, turn from the pain of broken promises, whispered words and lies, looking for suggestions, relief in unguent jars. Roses. Remember roses. The beads of sweat from Mohammed's brow. A brisk rub on the cheek with a crushed petal, some spit for added gloss, and the skin shines in response, the paleness from life gone.

Everyday, Shahida and her mother walked past the haveli, the sprawling mansion belonging to the nawab. Mother shook with a hacking cough, leaning against the acacia tree, inhaling crystals of camphor. She gave out a mousy smell of sickness, mildew spreading in the dark. "Please, mother, you need to rest. I'll go get the flowers."

Shahida ran to the compound wall growing glass shards on top. The glint of sunbeams splayed from glass to honey irises of her eyes. How she loved this place: the miniature onion-domed mosque, the multi-colored gardens. Stepping into the guardhouse, she pointed to her mother leaning against the tree outside. "I've come to fetch the fallen petals and roses," she said, balancing a wicker basket on a slender, protruding hip. She walked past the mosque to the garden beyond. From here, she got a good view of the zenana through lattice screens. In a far corner, a woman appeared briefly on a wooden balcony carved like a lace ruff. She stood and combed masses of inky hair. Beyond the cusped arches, other women reclined on silk cushions listening to poetery with far away eyes.

Shahida lifted red earth from a handful of petals and tossed the lot into her basket. Such roses, sweet cabbage faces. What wondrous work could be achieved in these gardens. And here they were, perfectly healthy women, lounging like lions in the sun, longing for something she could not see or understand. Piling her basket high, she was about to leave when she heard a man's voice. She saw the English hakim, Paul Glasgow, the doctor who bled the women in the house. His face was the color of the whitest flour. He had sky-trapped marble eyes. Shahida saw fat books in his hands.

"*Kholo, Kholo.* Open the gates," he commanded to the guards. What books, what mysteries lurked in the zenana's library, she wondered. Remembering the few tattered books that she arranged daily on the windowsill, she choked up inside. She saw herself growing old with her mother, the women of their house. An image of herself—matted hair and raving mind, tiny garden unkempt and overgrown. No, by the grace of Allah, she prayed, not such a fate. Help Shahida. Let there be another way.

༺࿔༻

The winds that bring the monsoon arrive, lifting dirt into eyes. The rain comes quietly at first, falling like tears. Then lightning. Now the rain falls steadily, soaking the ground. The sweaty smell of earth, sodden leaves and clumps of grass. On the window, rivulets, the way she begins, an angry trickle every month. Mother called and said, "It is time."

"Time for what?"

"Put your books aside. You must cover your face, your hair. Come, we must make plans."

"I feel no different. Just like myself." She pushed aside the veil mother held, staring at her with stubbornness, such unblinking eyes that they both laughed. The smell of plucked feathers wafted out of mother's skin. Shahida's pupils dilated as she heard her words.

"Next week, you'll go with the dancers to the haveli, the house of the nawab. We must prepare for your new life."

On his birthday, the nawab spent the afternoon in the zenana. The chief eunuch massaged his back with ebony rollers as he sat surrounded by wives and concubines. Rehana, his first wife, gave a nod. A slender woman paid her respects and began to sing in a nasal voice. She sang of lovers meeting secretly, parting with outstretched hands. The woman held out her own hand as if reaching out. She was an alluring sight. Her pearl necklace moved off center favoring the right breast. The nawab scratched his nose and waved her aside. Dressed in pastel yellow, the second one came forward with an offering, a gift of walnut juice extracted by her own hands. Others with silver basins and silken cloths lingered behind. Yellow woman brushed the dye into his eyebrows and hair. Her fingertips felt cool on his forehead. The nawab relaxed and closed his eyes. When he opened them again, the pit of her cleavage ran down his nose, ample mountains rising on either side. He pushed the woman away with the flat of his palm. He yawned and craned his neck, looking beyond the rustling women, a slight movement in the background catching his eyes. "Bring that woman to me," he ordered to the chief eunuch. He pointed to the group of nautch dancers that had entered the courtyard, the bold young one walking ahead of the group.

"Your humble servant Shahida," she said and dared to look up. These nautch dancers were not like the women in the harem. They revealed their faces to him and the world outside. The young one who stood before him, the way she carried herself, why this was no coquette, she seemed a little defiant, endearing somehow. "Are you here to dance for me?" he teased, ogling her perky chest.

"I am not a dancer. But the stories I tell—such strangeness that your hair would curl back. Like the poet Sadi of Persia, I walk the garden, speaking the language of leaves and flowers. Shahida will turn your head with the things she knows, the cures she can concoct. With such possibilities, I ask you, gracious nawab of Zarba, what would you like?"

"How about a surprise? Can you do that?" The nawab combed the whiskers on his chin with folded fingers, knuckles jutting out. A muffled murmur twisted between the women and eunuchs.

"I, Shahida, say that I am here to be your new wife. With me you will know such times that . . ." She gestured above the heads of the women seated around.

A peacock screeched for a long moment.

The nawab waved a many-ringed hand in the air. There was shuffling going on, everyone wondering what to do. Then a tiny, anxious voice.

"Is the nawab surprised?" Throwing his face to the heavens, the nawab howled, slapped his thighs.

"I wish to hear one of these stories you boast about."

Shahida spoke about the juice extracted from the soma, elixir of the Hindu Gods. Relatives painted viscous paste of the plant on a young widow, chanting of life beyond. To help the woman turn away from the burden of her body, they plugged nerves and pores, a numbing shield that kept flames outside. The widow saw her loved one waiting patiently, twirling the stem of the mythical blue flower, a champac. The monotonous sound and his image fused in her mind. She latched on to the incessant movement of his fingers, the wonder of him alive. The urge to travel became intolerable. Before stepping into the pyre, if the thought was of pain, that ugly assertion of the body, then the heat became real. So she remained unwavering, grabbing his hands, watching twin reflections of herself in his eyes. This was the ultimate opportunity to prove her power, the tossing of it all, leaping above life itself.

As the moon folded over from round to crescent that night, there was the hooting of owls, the braying of an ass. Sleeping women in the zenana shuddered in their sleep.

Servants entering the house at dawn saw that the new bride was already up. "Jasmine is best plucked before sunlight," she said. In the garden, Shahida laughed and stripped more and more of the vine. She smelled the scent between fingertips with half-closed eyes. Underneath her pillow maids collected the remnants, limp and brown.

Sometime in the middle of her first five years in the haveli, eunuchs say, her passion shifted and slanted more resolutely towards the rose. Shahida, they whispered in the marketplace, was like one possessed. Was it the nearness to her beloved gardens? Her mind worked like a beam, pointing to possibilities with a sudden light. She rested in the mornings, roaming ceaselessly in the dark. In the moonlight, petals plumped up, no chance of evaporation from harsh rays of the sun. She snipped red and reddest roses for intoxicating madness, yellow for its tang, white for a hint of bitterness. The wild pink one she favored for its delicacy. Shahida extracted rose water by double boiling, straining, diluting and concentrating the fluid till the effluvia was just right. This she poured into filigreed silver sprinklers with globular bodies and elongated necks.

⤳

Behind the carved sandalwood screen, a woman strummed the strings of the sitar. A mynah with a golden beak cocked its head this way and that. Lush rectangles of Kashmiri carpets spotted the floor. Preparing for the nawab's monthly visit, Shahida sat on a lacquered stool. Bits of smoking loban, that fragrant resin reminiscent of ripening pomegranates, curled through loose strands of her just-washed hair. Shahida covered her parting with a chain, a pendant with pearls in the middle of her forehead. Lifting a silver sprinkler, she carefully dabbed rosewater on her neck and wrists. Like nerves that travel from the ganglionic knots, she discovered that fragrance must be carefully applied in the center of the body, where temperature is maximum, absorption quick. Crushed and smeared in these spots, the perfume of flowers acts like a medium of character. Magnetic vibrations rise from centers and beam out, pulling complementary forces, drawing vitality from other souls, en rapport with planets.

Shahida sprinkled water on reed curtains of vetiver covering the windows in anticipation of an amorous night. As the nawab slept the sleep of the satiated, Shahida paced the floors. To trap the spirit of a rose so a drop, a whiff, carried one to another realm. How to extract the soul of a flower? The rosewater she distilled, the fragrance of it, was still diluted somehow.

She had exhausted the books in the library, turning page after page, looking for a way, a stray hint somewhere. Overcome with fatigue, she rested an elbow on a book in her lap and looked out. She saw the English *hakim* enter with guards. He came to bleed Rehana in four spots for a headache that rarely left. "Those fat books in his hands, are they his and what are they about?" Shahida asked the eunuch who spat betel juice in an arc.

They said Paul knew many languages from his travels, ways of other worlds.

Tossing globs of resin on the embers of the brazier, Shahida filled the nawab's chamber with thick, sweet smoke. The embers sputtered and rose, his face puffed with desire. As the moon faded for the sun, the nawab nodded his consent. So it was arranged that Shahida and Paul would exchange books and papers, speak and listen between silk curtains.

∽

In Paul's world infants curled inside cabbage leaves, strangers rose from parsley beds. The mystical language of flowers grew in garland stories in her head. From the tormented heads of blue-eyed lovers she learned that a rose sent in the upright position breathed both fear and hope; dreaded its return upside down, which meant too bad, don't fear nor hope.

"This recipe I hear about, to bring a lost one back, how does that work?" he asked in an amused voice.

She sighed and wrote, "It seems almost as if from another life." Paul cleared his throat, skimming over the ingredients.

"This special rose blood you speak of, do you have some of that?" Shahida gestured to the eunuch. Paul continued to read the rest. *Smeared on the forehead of the one left behind, the yearning, the heat from brainwaves, the scent from the recipe, these will blend and send out a strong call. Listen closely for footsteps before wiping the brow. Now go, greet him, forgetting the past.*

Shahida's bangles tinkled wildly as she sprinkled rose water on the curtain. A maddening smell rammed Paul's brain; his senses whirled. He wiped his face with a kerchief, inwardly swooning, weighing the possibilities of marketing such a find. If he were to speak, he thought, his voice would come out high pitched this time.

This, she said, of the rosewater, was just a first step. Had he heard about alchemists who mentioned the soul of a rose, sealed with tiger fat and simmered in a fire of husks? Paul was fascinated. The woman, clearly haunted, what if she were to succeed in her quest? He reached for his muslin kerchief and wiped his neck, front and behind.

Sensing his excitement, Shahida felt the mystery become doubly alive. For many following months, she thought he bled the women indifferently, anxious it seemed, only for their hour to arrive.

ᴄᴏ

Paul entered the garden with a copy of Materia Medica under his left arm, right hand swinging the question mark of his umbrella. Inside the top hat, the afternoon heat melted in a ribbon around his forehead. His woolen britches rubbed in wrong places. He inhaled briskly changing into a correct face.

From a distance, he could see that Shahida sat on the milky rim of the lotus pond, two mounds of sleeping servants on the ground. The awning of the verandah sheltered her from the glare. For her, only dumb animals and Englishmen gallivanted in the sun. Hair cascading in uninhibited fashion, she poured fistfuls of water and rose blood between toes. Frogs and fish swam close to the surface, dopey from the scent. Being a leg man, he gulped his saliva watching the curve of her foot, wetness shining on her nails, hearing a chorus of wind chimes. A vigilant mosquito aimed for his left lobe. The umbrella fell; he spanked his ear. Her veil slid as she turned, ringed thumb flying to shield her dough ear.

Watching her thus from afar, he left unseen, the forgotten book still cupped in his hand.

Next morning, as the awning was rolled up, the servant maid poured Shahida's bath water, gallons of rose blood, into the lotus pond. Floating on top, when Shahida came by with her thirsty toes, a net of green oil, base of attar, fake lily pad. She flung herself on the ground. Praise Allah, whose son Mohammed shed sweat from his brow on earth, rising as the rose. Salutations to the sun, magical light. There lies Mecca, showering a speck of a woman with such grace. In a dazed state, she fetched an empty bottle, swept the green net inside and sealed the top.

ᴄᴏ

Paul walked purposefully, positioning himself beside the curtain, like he always did. How to explain the moment of excitement, the mind losing itself? Shahida's arm reached through a slit in the silk, impatient for the book in his hand. Her chest was heaving slightly, breath uneven and fast. Her fingers brushed tiny hair above knuckles, the thick crescent of a nail. Holding the open book in one hand, she noticed he had signed his name, all curls and whorls, an incomprehensible tongue. She clenched and unclenched her other fist like a just-brushed sea anemone. The topaz eyes clouded, a nuance of a frown.

Next to his name, she used her quill dipped in patchouli ink to add a flower, a stem. Shahida's signature of passion. She trembled as if stirring inside. The moment expanded as it flew from the garden to noble, piercing eyes: the eunuchs engaged in gossip, Paul and Shahida face to veil, their fleeting touch.

Why had she not carried it patiently, this weight, clutching like a child? Perhaps it was madness like they said that had turned her head. Not one understood that religion of the mind, Shahida all along, observing herself.

The nawab and his first wife claimed the discovery as their own. Stories of wronged women, they said, multiplied like guppies in a pond. Who would people believe, the murmurings of a lone Englishman, traders who carried away shawls and spices, gaping at gems exclaiming "the size of apricots?"

Shocked by the way things turned out, Paul sat around and moped for a bit. He downed the last mouthful of a pukka glass of gin and roughly wiped the bottom of the glass on his thighs. What rot, he thought. It was too much. All this business about bloody smells. Frigging idiotic. Still he supposed, meeting the woman, finding out about attar, the art of perfume application, these had been worthwhile. Pity about the Begum, this place. It wouldn't do to get too attached. No harm done. One must think forward. How to instruct those charming and elegant creatures, the ladies of Europe.

In a few months, proof of Shahida's past sailed in a book to far flung land. A woman's signature of passion—petals unfurling, thorns on either side. On land, Begun Shahida's tale of attar remained with a handful of lowlifes in the bazaar—eunuchs, dancing girls, forgotten by the rest.

A Couple of Rogues

THE IDEA CAME TO SHANKAR while squatting in the outhouse. Being a creative sort, he understood the process and continued squatting long after it was necessary. It was a good ten minutes before the steps of the experiment lodged themselves firmly in his head. A methane gas plant at the village temple was not only innovative, it would solve all their current financial problems.

His wife Meenakshi stood before the tulasi, the sweet basil plant that occupied a prominent spot in the backyard. The cook handed him a second tumbler of coffee and Shankar gulped it down while he glanced hurriedly at the headlines of *The Hindu* before rushing for his bath. As he dipped and poured water over himself, he made a list of things he would need for a trial run. Drying himself, he carefully replaced the sacred thread around his neck. Hunching slightly, he peered into the mirror and applied vibuthi, holy ash, in three lines across the length of his forehead. He grabbed the cap of his toothpaste and smeared the edges with his wife's Vaseline. He pressed the sticky outline to the middle of his forehead. This he filled in with a bright red.

"I'm off to see Mani."

"What for?" she asked.

"It's all rather complicated. I don't have time to go into it now. We have to do something during the upcoming festival to collect funds, save the honor of the temple."

Meenakshi shook her head and muttered to herself. When he turned purposeful like this, she thought there was something strange cooking in his head. She wanted him to acquire dignity in old age, at least, she said, during the retirement years. He heard her curse the fate of her horoscope written sharply on her head. All those years in the city scrimping and saving, she complained, she just wanted some peace and quiet. "A little respect, as one of the senior couples in the village. Is that too much to ask?" she said.

∽

He locked his bicycle under the neem tree outside the courtyard. The temple elephant swayed, swinging its trunk this way and that before curling the tip around a bundle of grass, carrying it to the mouth. The trainer, Nayyar, stood there snorting snuff.

"Is Mani in?"

Wiping his nostrils with the towel on his shoulder, the trainer pointed to the sanctum sanctorium inside. Shankar waited outside the closed doors, listening to the tinkling of the bell as the priest finished his morning rituals of cleaning and decorating the dancing idol. The heavy doors creaked open and Mani came out, smelling sour in spite of his recent bath, bulging breasts shining with sweat.

In his right hand, he held the customary plate of offering. Shankar reached out with his palms to shield the camphor's flame, taking back the warmth, fingertips to eyes. "How much?" he asked, pointing to the slotted metal box, the hundi, where the worshippers dropped their offerings.

"About two thousand. What do you think?"

Shankar perked up. He outlined his plan of action. Mani's face crumpled. He became silent. "Trust me," assured Shankar. "The idea is solid. You'll accomplish everything—the grand show, the procession around the streets, an overflowing hundi, the advantage of electricity on a

87

Sunday morning—they'll be suitably impressed."

In the past, Shankar's experiments had produced minor problems. Of course, these had eventually been ironed out. Money was scarce and the temple needed help. He remembered their conversation two years ago, when Mani had first approached him for advice. "Times are changing, Mani," Shankar had said. "You need to liven up things here like Madras. You need music, special effects, the temple's own stall selling flowers and coconuts." The priest's eyes had rounded, eyelids batting wildly.

"Can we do all that?"

"Leave it to me," Shankar had said, wearing an expression worthy of his title, ex-emeritus professor of electrical engineering, AC College of Technology, Madras. He had taken the money and purchased a second-hand CD player from Ambika's Electronics in Palghat. Into the machine he had inserted a CD, fiddling with an extension cord, pushing the plug into a socket near the idol. Instantly, the place was transformed. Mani's mouse-like chanting was submerged with the dramatic beat of drums. The heavy walls vibrated with lively sound. People passing by had stopped in their tracks. A few went so far as to remove their footwear and go inside. The old woman who guarded slippers outside squatted firmly, planting a servile look in her eyes, motioning repeatedly to those peering curiously from the streets to come, visit inside.

The same day after sunset, the evening puja had drawn a big crowd. It was nobody's fault that the half-blind idiot Govindan had tripped the cord with his walking stick, shattering the drama of it all at the crucial moment, towards the end, as the little boys clanged the bells. Everyone noticed that Mani's voice squeaked more than before with the lack of background. Some of them opened their eyes, dropped folded palms and smiled. Still, it was nobody's fault that the only available socket was so close to where the faithful lined up.

Shankar's other invention was almost a success. The cracked sand-stone lingam beside the idol was replaced with a shiny, dark phallus in bronze. The design was ingenious, Mani had had to admit. The top part sat on grooves, fitting neatly onto the bottom half. The practically invisible hole on top and the fine chicken wire sieve around the bottom drained and collected the liquids underneath: milk, buttermilk, honey and ghee that Mani poured daily on the lingam. The temple had saved a bundle by recycling holy liquids.

For two blissful weeks, things went smoothly. After that, the rats had come. They chewed through the chicken wire at night. Mani discovered another flaw. The tulasi leaves and flower petals choked the fragile filter, making liquids leak out, mapping the stone steps, creating havoc on the floor below where sticky footprints were soon covered with ants.

ᏟᎤ

Shankar thought his affinity with the elephant was a definite asset to his new plan. When he came by with his everyday offering of two rather over-ripe bananas, the elephant dropped the palm frond, assuming a greeting stance. It probed the man's armpits and crotch savoring the familiar smell. Having made contact, it let out a rumble, irresolutely swinging the trunk, then curling, preparing to trumpet again. This bumptious twiddling went on and on till Shankar produced the bananas. Using the tip of the snout as a scoop, the elephant lifted the fruits efficiently. By the time Shankar left, the animal was busy scratching its rump, rubbing against the trunk of the nearest breadfruit tree with half-closed eyes.

This being October, a period of musth, the elephant was slightly in rut. Hurling balls of shit at the trainer, it had gathered the chains and fetters, piling them into a heap, and gone on strike. Nayyar said it refused to obey commands, ramming tusks into the trunk of the breadfruit tree, rolling crazy eyes. First thing in the morning the animal greeted him by tossing a breadfruit. Nayyar had been caught off-guard, his attempt to duck the flying fruit had failed. "Randy bastard," he had yelled, clutching his cheek now turning purplish black.

Shankar had just returned to the temple from the neighboring village where he had gone to visit an old friend. Seeing him, the trainer wrung his hands, saying, "I think we need the medicine. What do you think?" Shankar said to follow him.

He explained to Meenakshi that he was in a rush.

She ignored him and asked "What happened to you?" pointing to Nayyar's face.

"He threw a breadfruit at me," mumbled the man, stroking the sore spot.

"In musth again? That elephant is a rogue, that's what," she scolded as if the man was responsible for the condition, Shankar thought. She disapproved of the androgen tablets that were passed on to the trainer. "Tampering with nature, that's what it was." Like most others in the village, Shankar realized, she believed seminal fluid to be vital for health. "Sacrilege," she said. "Whoever heard of stuffing a Siva temple elephant with hormones? I want no part of the plan." Watching Nayyar flinch as he tried to speak, she went inside, grumbling to herself. "May Siva forgive you your sins," she said to Shankar as he folded the envelope. She handed Mani two extra bananas, being the good Hindu woman she was. Perhaps she believed that would atone for his chemical indiscretion, Shankar thought.

Her contribution to the elephant's well-being was an herbal concoction she made with other women. Shankar watched as they mixed oils of garlic, camphor and gardenia. She instructed Nayyar to dilute and pour the paste, it was a natural insect repellent and antiseptic for sensitive skin. She said herbal medicine was better; one knew what went into such things. "Mysterious hormones that one couldn't decipher, that's something else," she muttered. Looking at her face, catching the fleeting scorn, Shankar could match the words to her thoughts. What to do? Does a husband listen to a wife? Men were stubborn goats. She had given up long ago. Shankar tried to distract and calm. He described the photograph of a wonderful lamp he had seen in his friend's house.

"An American magazine," he enthused, hoping to impress. She snorted in reply.

⌒

Mani and Shankar came out of the temple with the feeling that all sorts of things were possible, the plan was airtight. The elephant stood on pillar legs while Nayyar filed his nails. The animal was the color of stone,

90

whooshing urine by the gallon. Testing the wind with his single finger, the elephant picked up the towel on Nayyar's shoulder and laid it on a branch. "Fetch that back," scolded the trainer. The two watching men suppressed a smile.

The carbon steel drums were delivered the following week. Nayyar wasn't sure that four were enough. The animal defecated twenty times a day, the quantity was enormous. He got hold of urchin boys who shoveled the mounds all day long. "Make sure they leave space on top," warned Shankar, covering half his face with a towel, holding his breath as he supervised. He inspected the funnel lids that went on top. "The idea is similar to a compost heap," he explained to Mani as the rotund man watched. The sagging drums were left to dry in the sun. Being a stickler for hygiene, the priest said he resented the swarms of flies in the compound.

Back at the house, Meenakshi had heard the news. "This fascination with elephant dung," she asked, "who are you trying to impress?" Standing before him, she slapped her forehead. "Because of you, I can't step out of the house. They're laughing. They think you're a lunatic," she gestured with her hands.

"Who's laughing?" he thundered and proceeded to the front door. He unlocked the bolt and looked to left and right. "I don't see anyone. You're becoming neurotic, that's what. I'll send for the taxi tomorrow. Why not go visit your grandchildren in Madras?" Meenakshi stopped her protests immediately.

"Why not?" she said, "I've been wanting to see the children for a while. October in the city is a wonderful time. All those weddings to attend and people to see." A dreamy look settled in her eyes. "Send for the taxi. You do that," she agreed. "I'll leave instructions with the cook."

He had not expected her to agree to leaving so fast. It was just fine with him, he consoled himself. He could carry out his plan without interference from a nagging wife. If Meenakshi wasn't around, he thought, he'd convert the bore-well motor to a generator and drive the turbine. She fussed about ample water for her bath, washing her hair daily, as if anyone cared about an old woman's gray hair.

A moment of contentment came over him after dinner though he'd cursed earlier when the power went off. The hissing gas lamp had a lulling effect, his eyes grew accustomed to the softer light. He dozed on and off sitting in his easy chair. He woke up scratching, devoured by mosquitoes that attacked with renewed energy realizing there was no ceiling fan. The power cuts were insane, he had to agree with his wife. She was sitting by the threshold, waving a gaudy Japanese style plastic fan. "It will be lonely without you," he mumbled grudgingly, eagerly searching for a sign. She continued fanning herself, first the face, then her neck which she extended by lifting her chin.

"You won't even know I'm gone; I see no difference whether I'm here or there," she said and sighed. Shankar knew his sixtieth birthday was coming up, a time to renew wedding vows. She had hinted about coral beads for a chain around the neck.

The tablets had taken effect, the elephant's behavior turned tractable again. The animal's dark shape and loose skin cloaked his manliness, the belly sagging again as he gobbled up everything in sight. Shankar noticed he was wallowing in mud, bathing with dust. The mosquitoes and fleas were numerous after the rains.

～

On the day of the festival, Shankar saw that Meenakshi and the other women sat surrounded by baskets of flowers. They unwound bundles of banana fiber casting on with deft fingers, knotting together lotus petals, roses and other flowers. Young girls sat to one side jabbing stems of jasmines with needles and stringing them with twine. The scent of roasting vermicelli swam through the air. Street vendors flaunted a strange combination of knick-knacks: iridescent bangles, khaki mountains of henna, cone-shaped packets of peanuts wrapped in childish handwriting that outlined steps to theorems from last year's class, crepe paper elephant kites with streaming snout tails that waved when the wind picked up and wobbly spools of kite-thread reinforced with glass dust.

He caught up with Nayyar and the elephant as they walked towards the pond. The elephant bathed for an hour. The trainer scrubbed the tusk, the smoothened worn right one (the elephant was right-handed) with a clump of coconut fiber, murmuring endearments all the time. Drops of water clung to the stiff bristles of the animal's chin. He rested his trunk on the upturned sharp left tusk, relishing every minute of the ritual, knowing it was a time for man and elephant to bond.

Walking back to the temple, Shankar noticed that the old woman guarding slippers outside sat by the pavement with glazed eyes. Her pierced earlobes drooped dramatically, grazing shoulders, stretched with decades of supporting chunky weights. The same fate seemed to have overtaken her breasts, they curtained her navel as she squatted on the mud. Her concave stomach, trained to fill easily with steaming tumblers of tea, rumbled in protest for a bit of rice. Her grandchild had made a basket of burrs. This she filled with bruised flowers which Meenakshi and the other women chucked out. Oblivious to the threads of snot that streamed down her childish face, she offered the container to her grandmother.

Later in the morning, crowds began to arrive. Shankar lifted the end of the PVC pipe snaking out of the drum. His nose twitched in anticipation, he took a deep breath. He felt like the captain of a relay race. He plugged in the open end to the valve of the gas cylinder. This, in turn, was connected to the makeshift boiler and gas burner. A gleaming brass vessel normally used for storing water had been loaned from the temple kitchen. The priest and the cook had objected to the use of the kitchen vessel, it wasn't as if this was cow dung. He pacified them by camouflaging the vessel with a coating of mud.

Shankar waited impatiently as the pressure built up, planting piercing eyes on the turbine and generator. It was only a matter of minutes before the leads sizzled to life. The filaments inside the lingam gave off a steady warmth. The turbine blades revolved, the generator roared, the crowd watched as the music turned deafening, Mani chanting at a high pitch. Shankar took off his glasses and wiped his face with his sleeve. The crowd stilled their shuffling feet. The wax coating on the lingam liquefied, the phallus responded with grief. The faithful watched the liquid trickle down, slapped their cheeks gently with palms in penance, for who understands the ways of Siva's wisdom, they were mere mortals, small creatures in the end.

Catching Meenakshi's face, Shankar nodded conspiratorially. He thought she slapped her cheeks harder. How many more births? her face read. Will the cycle never end? What kind of destiny was this that had made her marry a clown?

This elephant is going to be a star, Shankar thought. Meenakshi had lovingly patched the small tears in his shiny clothes. The mended brocade sheet looked majestic on his back. Leather harnesses of bells were wrapped around the legs, a useful warning for fools like Govindan. A velvet cape with scattered copper domes encircled the forehead. Nayyar tied a necklace of satin red rope with a big bell pendant around the neck. Pompoms made from yak hair bobbed up and down. The elephant's leafy ears waved in and out, driving away those pesky flies.

Nayyar's sons had assignments. The trainer was excited, a big day for man, sons and elephant. The older boy looked clearly bored; elephant duty was not on his mind. All those girls on the street below, a fine time to be pushing and shoving, smiling back at pretend severe looks in their eyes. Why did the brat grin and sway, adolescent exaggeration, Shankar surmised. The boy's noisy friends whistled and watched. He went up to them, suggesting decorum, the procession was about to begin, couldn't they see that? They said they felt sorry for the elephant, pestered with all those clothes and accessories, not to worry, they had fixed that. They laughed raucously and left, scattering in different directions. Shankar's experienced nose detected toddy breath. Had Nayyar's son imbibed? He saw that the elephant had stopped reaching out with his trunk, was standing unnaturally still. He recalled that the animal loved sweet, smelly wine.

Surrounded by her friends, Meenakshi was chattering, looking a little in musth herself. Shankar winked at her and grinned as she blushed. He knew that look. She'd do more than talk about coral beads tonight. Shankar and the elephant ambled out of the temple, he with a smug look about the eyes, the giant swaying his tender arm, a silly dolphin smile around the mouth. He heard the priest's voice, shrilly with delight, the trainer inhaling loudly, lungs coated with a film of snuff.

Nayyar's older son held the dancing idol on the wobbling back, the younger boy sat fanning the holy face with peacock fans. The trainer occasionally opened and closed a silk parasol trimmed with glittering thread. The priest and his assistants chanted in front. Approaching the fancy corner house, Nayyar commanded the elephant to halt. The family promised a large donation, Mani had been notified.

The camphor was lit and a plate was prepared with coconut and flowers, a return offering to the generous man and lady of the house. Shankar saw the elephant shift his weight wildly as if a maddening itch spread between the legs. No, he thought, the animal seemed to be contemplating the interesting looking pillars in front of the house. Yes, the columns possibly reminded him of tree trunks. The animal turned around; the crowd screamed. The owner of the house and his wife gasped; the elephant reached out to grab. It was a while before he let the pillar go, heeding Nayyar's gentle tongue. Then the animal lay his snout on his tusks, becoming very still, preparing for a nap.

An hour of waiting, the crowd grew restless. The idol was removed, Nayyar and his sons dismounted in disgust. The elephant refused to react, he froze statue-like. Mani gesticulated and yelled hysterically at Nayyar. People were leaving. What about the coins and notes in his slotted box? The sleepy elephant picked up the priest deftly and deposited him on the roof of the house. The remaining children watched in awe. Mani grabbed the weather vane, the circling bird squeaked in response. Shankar felt deeply for his friend. The priest's expression was variegated: the shock of the height, the feel of elephant skin, the sharp metal wing in his hand. Mani almost fainted, his towel slipping, the two mounds on his chest pointing towards the sky. Walking women stopped and laughed.

cᢣᢣ

For Shankar the drama exploded into the night. The suspense of Meenakshi's pinched face, the silent treatment in bed. He kissed her fingers, promising to make up for the honeymoon they'd never had. He stuck his nose in her hair, saying softly, "Did you wash it again tonight?" She turned around innocently, targeting a fast knee, ripping his lust. No sorry, did it hurt, not a trace of regret. Acknowledging herself, she spilled the shame, the fate of being a coot's wife. Fooling around with shit drums, lecherous elephants, snuff-snorting types, a couple of rogues, she wailed, mourning with red eyes. Her fingers clasped and tugged the corner of his pillow. Who was this—his thumb-sucking grandson or his wife? She moved nearer, anticipating the contour of his body, this woman of mercury, his wife. No experiments, he swore, not outside the house.

✑

"We never do anything together," Meenakshi said, "What about Sanskrit lessons?" Now that life here was organized he thought, she worried about the next.

"Yes," he managed in a muffled tone, "arrange for anything digni-fied."

Mani worked alone, squeaking for hours, dissipating fat. "Poor man," Meenakshi said, "save the bananas for him."

Shankar noticed that the beggar woman in front of the temple lost her servile look. "No one came anymore, the temple was ordinary," she said. She was thinking of leaving, this village was a dead loss.

Meenakshi made him dizzy, folding the newspaper, massing maga-zines, fattening cushions on the divan, straightening the slant of his cal-endar on the wall. She snarled a command at the cook who stood staring out the window with idiot eyes. Shankar saw that she had combed out the snarls and piled her freshly washed hair. A few tendrils had dodged the pins, tumbling about on the nape of her neck, "I've asked for the jeweler to come in the afternoon," she said. "It's childish to procrastinate in our stage of life." He turned smoothly, detour on his tongue.

"Do you remember the light for the bedroom I talked about?" She played on, pretending to be deaf.

"Mani will be here any minute," she said, handing him the fruit. He looked up and shook his fist, a banana drill, piercing the sky.

The priest, his swelling chest hidden seductively under a honey-combed cotton towel, instructed in a monotone. Shankar tried hard to listen, he even picked up a pencil and followed the lines. Between the verses of the Geeta, he drafted a plan. He designed an American light for the bedroom, recalling details of the picture in his mind. When he had told Meenakshi about lights in America that turned on and off when someone clapped, she had dismissed it as foolish, irrelevant for their life. "We don't have to clap, just blink—and the lights go off. Perhaps America is a big country, they need all that noise. Forget about lights with ears, why not design lights that shine?"

Always the smart one, not easily impressed. What to do? Does a wife listen to a husband? Women were silly sparrows. He had given up long ago. He had hoped that she would acquire some kindness, at least during this time. A little kindness, some love, was that too much to ask? "Would a sane woman go around clapping in the dark?" she had said. "Stark raving mad. Most women marry men. Only I married a fool." He looked at her and watched her snort.

Kneading his stomach, Shankar got up and walked. Life was impossible inside, better lived in the outhouse.

Bat Soup

SHE UNDID THE CHILDISH KNOTS of the cloth and dropped the bats on the floor. A smoky smell of singeing flesh filled the hut. Flapping wings lay flat, edges blackened, burnt borders, a crisp outline. Ma picked them up, lifting by the ears. Sitha began to talk but her mother was traveling, eyes out the window, seeing somewhere else. Ma had enough to think about these days, the baby growing inside and Pa in jail. Sitha did not mention anything about the woman at the temple. The woman, she remembered, stood waving by the entrance, the mouth of Angkor Wat.

It has been more than two hours since Robona went to fetch lotus seeds from the pond. Sitha thinks her sister useless, a dreamer, that one. She has seen her there before. Filling her scarf to sagging level quickly, she lingered, reluctant to leave water behind. She nicked at stalks with the long nail of her thumb. Then she brought the flowers home in a bunch for Ma. "See here," she said, "Isn't it so beautiful?" Ma usually said nothing. Then Sitha turned to her sister, made a face and danced her tongue about. Ma knew Robona had waded in and out of the pond, collecting lotuses, playing with shrimp, staring at nothing, anything, pretending, watching young boys with hooded eyes. Things were not the

98

same like before; Ma so sad, her sister always going out.

Sitha noticed how Robona walked since she turned sixteen. She wound her sarong tightly, pulling at the edges before tucking in. Then when she walked, she swayed just a little, thighs brushing, small, tight buttocks seesawing, so glad to be alive. Sitha has seen her sister's private mirror hidden under the bamboo coil of the sleeping mat. It has a wooden frame and isn't cracked. Ma's mirror on the wall has a crack that bursts into a star. Sitha has to move away from the middle, more to one side. Ma didn't want her girls carrying snot threads, she was particular about things like that. In the mornings, Sitha remembered to use the edge of her towel to clean ears and nose, then washed her clothes by beating them on rocks.

Watching Ma toss in the washed bats, one by one, into the boiling pot, she pulled the stool, let the crutch rest against a bamboo pole and sat near the bush outside. She felt the pocket of her cotton frock and pulled the bulge out. The woman at the temple had given it to her. She had broken off a triangle and offered it, popping one into her own mouth. The white pyramid box said TOBLERONE. The letters remained still and slanting, red outlined in gold.

Sitha had always thought chocolate had to be brown. This one was milky, bits of nuts peeping out. It felt all warm and syrupy, the way it glided down. Sweetness coated the tongue for a very long time.

The woman had walked towards her, a metal crutch under her arm. This was odd, Sitha thought, for she had both legs. She watched as the woman popped the crutch open, a metal man on the ground. Then she stuck in a shiny face on top, a single glass eye. "Camera," she said, showing teeth to Sitha. The woman had hair the color of hay, eyes so green they were those of a cat. They reminded Sitha of paddy fields in the sun. Sitha saw this color when the sun was bright and she closed her eyes. When she opened them again, the color of paddy was cool, like the woman's eyes. Sitha had done this that afternoon in the field, the day she had stepped on that terrible thing, what the woman called a mine. Poor Theng. He stood behind her and that was the last day she had seen him alive.

⌒

Sitha remembered that day last year when she and Theng had a fine time. Robona had been nagging all morning: "Sitha! Sitha! Remember your promise to Ma. Time to feed the chicken. Sitha!" The thin afternoon air hoisted Robona's request and carried it, past two kapok trees, flying with her voice. Sitha heard it right away. Shell ears. The sound of the world always in the background, all through the games.

A few, quick words and her friends were running behind her, bare, brown feet kicking up dust. All of them and Theng huddled in front of her stilt house.

"Wait here. Just a few minutes. I'll be back," she said.

Underneath the house, she pushed open the lid of the seed bucket. A small plastic pail with a white handle hung from a nail nearby. She dipped this in the grain and turned to walk out. The birds were smart. They surrounded her in a hurry. She saw one squat and lay an egg by the bush. In the middle of the ground before the house, she scattered the seeds around. The birds' necks moved according to chicken rhythm, pecking and pecking, swallowing the grains.

"Is that you Sitha? Where were you? What took you so long? Still playing with those midget friends?" Robona spoke from the outdoor bath, the sound of her voice escaping through the open ceiling, the cracks and holes woven into the diagonal pattern of the bamboo walls. She had left a pile of clean clothes; a sarong, her favorite *kramar* that she tied often around her head, and a cotton blouse, all folded neatly along with her towel, on a stool beyond the plywood door.

Sitha heard her friends on the street. Somebody was laughing at a whispered joke. She watched Theng break away from the circle and then he stepped ahead. He whistled and waved: Hurry! Staring him down with a scowly face, she pressed a finger to her lips. Ssshh! Sitha walked towards her sister in the bath and peeked through the holes. She saw her sister soaping her nose, cheeks, fingers rubbing all over her face, eyes tightly shut. Since Robona grew breasts like Ma, hair down there, Sitha found her sister has lost all sense of fun. The splash of water against a body; a rooster crowing suddenly. Then the stillness of the afternoon air. Sitha looked up. Thick branches of a mango tree line the ceiling of the bath. A map of green and blue, shaded veins and light. Soaping her face Robona fussed, so grown up. "I'll tell Ma when she comes from the market. You'll be punished—wait and see."

"I heard you already. I'm feeding the chicken. I'll finish before I go," Sitha said.

She made an ugly face at Robona; she stuck her tongue out and danced it all about. Then she pushed the plywood door of the bath quietly up and to the side so the latch was undone. Her sister was rubbing the skin on her knees, still closing her eyes. In Sitha's pocket, Theng's gift wiggled against a thigh. A lily pad colored frog. Snaky brown lines. Bulging pebble eyes. She tapped the frog's head with her forefinger, a signal for don't jump. Then she picked the soap bar off the floor and let it rest on the clothes' pile outside. She lifted the frog from her pocket and dropped him into the soap container. She closed the door.

Sitha watched through the holes. Robona reached for the soap.

"Eeeee! Eeeee! A scream like a bird. Lily pad jumped and jumped trying to escape.

Through with her splashing and scolding, Robona's hand emerged quickly, an elephant snout, Sitha thought, grabbing the pile of clothes, lifting inside in a flash. The soap fell to the ground. It was covered with mud. Robona was in a lot of trouble with Ma, dirtying a new bar of soap like that.

Sitha grabbed the frog, now near her feet. She ran towards Theng and they sped across the street. Her other friends also ran, seeds lifted by the wind. Squatting behind a bush, looking through gaps between leaves, she saw Robona come out from the bath. She watched as her sister clenched and shook a fist in the air. Next to Sitha, Theng was squirming and stuffing the frog into his shirt. They had agreed to take turns, keep him from the adults. Robona was looking everywhere, mouthing words to herself. She looked so foolish talking to nobody in particular.

Sitha watched her climb the steps, then disappear inside the house. Robona would tidy up the only room in the house, boil water on the primus stove for thick, sweet tea. Ma would be home soon. Perhaps Ma had a good day at the market; all the mangoes in her basket gone. Sitha imagined the ching ching of Ma's cloth coin hip bag as it bounced this way and that. Fish and vegetables for dinner. Perfect with sticky rice.

Robona shouted from the window of the stilt house. "Ho! Sitha! Sitha! I can see you hiding. Wait and see. I'll get you this time."

It was time to go. Sitha knew she must get ready for Ma. She tapped her forefinger on Lilypad's head protruding between the buttons on Theng's shirt. Good-bye, pebble eyes. You sweet jumping thing. Straightening from the squatting position, she reminded Theng, "Don't forget to bring the frog. He is mine when we play near the paddy fields."

They agreed to meet at the usual spot, under the old kapok tree.

Theng asked, "Will Ma let you come? Your sister allow?"

"Yes. Yes. Under the tree in a couple of hours. I'll be there you see."

Past the clucking chickens in front of her house, she closed the plywood door of the bath. She shoved a piece of stem in place to secure the loose latch. In case Robona had ideas of revenge. After her bath, Sitha came out wearing her cotton lotus color frock. The lucky one Pa gave last year for her ninth birthday. Inside the house, Robona was standing in the corner, examining her face in the mirror. She was using the private mirror she hid under the bamboo coil of the sleeping mat. As Sitha combed her hair, using Ma's mirror, she had to move away from the middle, more to one side. The tangles hurt. A tooth of her comb snapped and bent as she tugged at her hair. Soon, Sitha's arms were tired from braiding at the back. The smell of kerosene was very strong though Robona had turned the stove off. She was there in the cracked mirror, standing behind, asking "You want me to do that?"

Sitha nodded her head and said softly, "When you go to the pond, I can wash the clothes if you like."

Robona replied, "You are a strange one. Enjoying frogs, beating clothes on rocks."

"It would give you more time to watch those boys."

"I do not watch boys."

The girls locked eyes in the mirror for a silent moment and then laughed and laughed.

"I am hungry. I want some tea," Sitha said.

"Can you wait a little, Ma will be home soon."

Sitha thought of Theng with Lilypad. It made her sad to think of him in the streets all day long, biting into a stale, crusty bun he had stolen from a bakery near the market. She asked Robona, "Do you think Ma will let me take something for Theng? A little rice, a dab of *niok mam* sauce?"

"Why do you worry about that fellow? He knows how to look after himself. You know what my friends said? Somebody saw him steal a bunch of bananas and eat without stopping. Imagine that. Don't waste your pity on that one, Sitha. You know what Pa says, we must learn to be hard to survive. Especially now. With the baby coming . . ." Robona finished the braids and Sitha tied them up with red nylon ribbons. In the place of hunger there was this funny feeling in her stomach. It was like the time she and Theng had stolen boiled watermelon candy and almost got caught. As if talking to herself, Robona said, "A baby coming. You know what that means."

"Maybe it won't be so bad. Maybe Ma won't be sick this time," Sitha replied.

∽

Last time, things had been bad. Ma lay curled and crying for weeks. Robona and Sitha had to go to the market in Ma's place, sharing her load in two baskets. The pills from the doctor used up a lot of money, Pa said, floating chicken eggs in a bowl of water to separate the good ones from the bad. The healthy ones danced as they floated; the bad ones sighed and sank. The girls had two slices of bread and tea in the morning, a bun again sometimes at night. The unceasing rains last year softened the vegetables in the vegetable patch. The water had drowned Pa's field, swept away the seedlings. Pa and his farmer friends sat in a circle and drank fermented palm liquor. Ma swallowed her pills and lost herself to everyone, lying on the mat, facing the wall.

One day, "I am hungry. I want some fish and rice," Sitha had cried.

Pa heard her cry and came in from outside. He walked up to her and slapped her hard. His fingers left red stripes on her cheek. Robona had spread coconut oil on her skin, crinkling her eyes as she saw that Sitha felt fresh the sting of Pa's slap. That was when Sitha realized that her sister and she were on the same side. Even Ma had done nothing. She continued to face the wall and cry. Next morning when Sitha woke, Pa greeted her in the morning with mangosteen segments in his palm. He asked for her to ride with him in the buffalo cart. He even gave her a coin for red nylon ribbons she wanted from the shop.

"Sitha, my Sitha," he called her all morning, every chance he got.

That day in the evening, Ma had grilled fish on the stove, cooked vegetables and rice. "It will be all right," Robona said, "When Ma has the baby next time, we can bully it, take turns, first me, then you. Only let's try not to fight in front of Ma and Pa." The food in Sitha's stomach lulled her into a short, deep sleep.

The following day, Theng showed her how to hunt for bats. They ran to the temples, climbed the walls like monkeys, scraping and scratching the skin on their knees.

෴

In the paddy fields, Sitha sometimes saw and heard things others did not. The images and sounds were first in her head and then outside. She heard small fish swim then looked down to see them glide between the rice roots. A bulge in her thoughts and there was a slit in the water, made by a sand crab. The sound of bubbles popping on the surface of paddy field water before tadpoles jumped out.

One day, it would later become that terrible day, she saw and heard nothing, only Theng. Theng before her eyes, his voice in her head. They held hands and splashed the water from the field on Lilypad. Until the moment she stepped on the land mine and fire came out of the ground like a fountain killing Theng and shattering her leg, until that moment, on that terrible day, Sitha and Robona shared secrets like sisters; she heard fish swim, roots grow; heard Ma and Pa sigh and love each other at night.

A month later, they took Pa away, called him a thief. They put him in jail.

☙

Inside the house, Ma stared into the bat soup bowl, Pa's face inside. Sitha slapped the bush outside with her soup. Better that the baby died again like the last time. Better not to voice aloud everything you thought. When it began to rain, she came inside. Lying on the mat, she watched raindrops slide down long leaves, the way Robona used to say she'd begin, angry trickles every month.

Sometimes, in the middle of afternoons, Sitha stood under the strangler fig tree and watched the color behind the eyes. Hearing cousins climb the tree and shout, she jumped with them, elastic muscles, strong thighs, phantom sheath over her mind. She skipped rope, skirt opening and closing like an umbrella, toes stabbing mud.

Tomorrow, when she stood under the strangler fig tree, she would imagine tadpoles tickling two long legs in the pond. She would remember her meeting with the woman by the entrance of Angkor Wat. She would dip into her cotton frock and pull a small piece of Toblerone out. She would press a milky triangle to a secret pocket of her mouth. Sucking slowly, all warm and syrupy, she'd forget everybody, making chocolate soup all by herself.

Traveling

THE EDGE OF THE WING SLICED a cloud. Pauline leaned back like the man in front, grateful for the window seat, slipping off her shoes, looking at the sky. The flight would take more than twenty-four hours, stopping at Honolulu and Guam before reaching Manila. Until today, she only read about faraway places in books, listened to stories from friends. She thought of the adventure ahead, she and Ray in exotic Manila, discovering new sides of each other after all this time. She had said no to the smiling stewardess when she came round with plaid blankets. Her own favorite shawl covered her lap, ivory with turquoise embroidery, tassels flying, doll's ponytails, attacked by gusts from the vent above. She watched her husband bend over, dip into his attaché case and come up with a sheaf of papers. Two years before retirement and Ray had landed an overseas assignment, a fitting finale to his curriculum vitae.

She must have dozed for a few hours. The movie was over, most of the lights were off. Outside, the sky was a canvas of black. A baby was crying at the back of the plane. Her mouth felt filmy. She reminded herself to use the bathroom in the early part of the journey, later was dicey business, people wet the seats with water, God knows what else. She prolonged the walk along the aisle by taking small steps, Japanese style.

It felt good to stretch knees. The baby that had been crying before was sucking from a bottle. The mother looked terrible, eye mask dangling like a bib, eyes glazed like she couldn't believe she had produced the weight on her lap. She remembered Jesse, her daughter in Maine, her baby granddaughter she wouldn't see or hold for a whole twelve months.

Outside the airport in Manila, Pauline stared at animated brown faces, belching cars, traffic, noise. The air was humid and heavy. There were blending odors of sweat and rotting fruit. The driver piled their luggage in the office car. Compared to Ray, the driver was small, his inky hair pomaded into place. He must have felt her eyes on him, for he turned around, raised eyebrows and smiled. She saw that he had a few gold capped teeth. Tucked into the air-conditioned coolness of the car, they drove away past all those lively brown faces. New England was a world away, the endless winter, the weight of wet snow on the shovel. She saw herself there, hugging the burn of thawing ears, swearing to get away from it all, dreaming of tropical nights, iguanas, sweat trickling between breasts.

♾

In the hotel room, she sipped pineapple juice. She looked up at ginger flowers on the dresser. The base of spikes the color of onion skin, climbing to watery coral, ending with a jolt of striped peach or pink. In the hotel lobby, they had walked past men skating on coconut husks, spreading wax on parquet floors.

Glancing at her watch, she realized the country club in Connecticut would be just opening at this hour. Back in the States, most weekends, they played golf with friends, Mike and Sandra. The weekend before they left, the four of them got into the cart outside the clubhouse. Ray was telling Mike about the Asian Bank, how he had landed the plum assignment for a year. Pauline told Sandra that her application for sabbatical had been approved, the principal of the private school where she taught English had found a substitute.

"Does it hurt?" Mike had asked, seeing Ray rub his swollen arm, the spot where he had his cholera shot.

"What about Pepto-Bismol, tetracycline, fly paper?" This was Sandra to Pauline. She had memorized checklists from travel magazines.

"I hear the women are fine," Mike winked at Ray.

"It's the skin and hair. All that fish they eat," said Sandra.

Pineapples and papayas, Pauline thought, flashing a dreamy smile.

"Bound to be interesting," Ray said, squatting, appraising the distance to make the putt, tugging at unruly blades of grass.

Sandra said to Pauline in a stricken voice, "Traveling to Europe for the holidays is one thing, but a year—twelve months—in the Philippines?"

Mike and Sandra went to Ireland every year. Their idea of travel was limited to the temperate zone, the comfort of the familiar.

⌒

"A lovely bungalow with a swimming pool," Mrs Carmen Santos, the landlady said. Peeking into the changing room nestled under a tree, Pauline was impressed. She entered a Somerset Maugham story, the lush vegetation alluring and unnerving at the same time. The previous tenants had had a cook, driver and a maid. "If you like," Mrs Santos said, "they can come with the house."

Pauline brushed up on local history from books she'd bought, discovering Filipino freedom fighters, Rizal, his Noli Me Tangere, the underground novel that started it all. She was moved and impressed by it, the photograph of the tiny author in a tuxedo on the book jacket, his European education, his shrewd technique of tucking Spanish colonial hypocrisy in the pages of a novel. She wondered if she should take lessons in Spanish. There were good mestizo teachers around.

The following week, at an afternoon coffee party, surrounded by international expat wives, she couldn't hide her enthusiasm, questioning non-stop. "Have you seen Fort Aguinaldo? Wonderful, isn't it? And the Lent processions I hear about. Are they really something to watch? Tell me, is it true they whip themselves?"

Her German hostess assumed an amused expression and leaned forward. She related a frightening incident that had happened months back.

"Headlines in the *Manila Times*," she said. "Two men, strangers, watching each other in the lobby of a hotel, Intercontinental, if I recall. Suddenly, one of them whips out a gun and shoots the other. Said the man had been staring too hard. Imagine! I'd always thought this cosmopolitan suburb, Makati, at least here it was safe, who knows, terrible things happen everywhere. Just luck, I suppose, that one is still alive."

"You mean the man killed him in the lobby, in front of a lot of people?" Pauline asked.

"No. It happened well past midnight. There were hardly any people around."

Surely it didn't apply to her and Ray, Pauline thought, their life. People had no business going out at all hours. They had always lived quietly, even in the States, not socializing much except with Mike and Sandra.

"We wouldn't dream of venturing out at such hours," Pauline said. These women have been away from home too long, she thought. One lost perspective being away, made up things to console oneself. The headlines in the States didn't comfort or deny dissolution. Didn't they know it wasn't safe to step out anywhere? By the time she looked up and tried to catch the eye of the German hostess, Pauline could sense she was tuned into the peripheral talk, so many tanned women yakking about shopping in Hong Kong. What did one say to them? She racked her brain and gave up, walking towards the dining table, nibbling at olives, pineapple bits, admiring the floral arrangement with cropped palm fronds. When she joined the women again, talk centered around the locals, it became them and us.

つ

Ray traveled constantly, overseeing feasibility studies, supervising dams and power plants. He peered at numbers in the evenings. "Budget figures," he said. Then he lay exhausted, the way he did now, flopping by her in old Bermuda shorts. His paunch seemed to be growing. When did his skin turn leathery? Pauline glanced at her own hands. Her freckles scattered all over. Inside or outside, the light here never held anything back. Ray blew a nasal whistle, beginning to snore. Watching him lying in bed next to her like that, tucked within himself, she hated him just a little but the feeling passed. She wondered if he left the air-conditioned rooms when he traveled, discovering something else?

Sitting on a wrought iron chair Sunday evening Pauline asked, "What do you do on your trips, I mean, other than work?"

"In Bangkok, I played some golf. And I went shopping for Thai silk, you know that. I almost got up the nerve to drink some snake blood, then I chickened out." Pauline was half listening, remembering that length of silk. It had hit her the moment he unpacked. Ray's idea of her was so far. Didn't he know she hated anything shiny, something that announced? She'd end up recycling it she thought immediately, disturbed by his choice. "Did you hear what I said?" he repeated.

"I heard. You couldn't bring yourself to drink snake blood." She could see the whisky was getting to him, he embellished badly at this hour.

They had planned a long weekend in Baguio, a hill station north of Manila.

In the fairway, the caddie and Ray walked together, she followed behind. The caddie wore stark white clothes next to chocolate colored skin. He walked gracefully, almost skipped, as if he was a dancer, as if his feet didn't quite touch the ground. Her eyes began to hurt from the glare. She would have liked to tell Ray she was thirsty, she felt a stitch on her side. The iced water the caddie carried looked slightly brown, she felt unsure. Ray took long steps when he walked, playing seriously, shushing her when she tried to talk. She didn't see what the fuss was all about, squatting and peering, appraising clubs, it would be easier if they'd hurry up, get the damn thing in. It wasn't as if daring or swiftness was involved, like skiing or jai alai. Ray looked self-satisfied. Perhaps he thought the caddie was awed by his shots; the solid drives, swiftly tumbling putts.

"Your grip is all wrong," he pointed out to her. He recommended easing up a little, stop elbows from flying so much. "Feel it like a buggy whip," he said.

After eighteen holes, Ray asked the caddie to join them at the bar. "What is a buggy whip?" he asked Ray. Pauline laughed. As empty amber bottles of San Miguel beer piled up, the caddie became animated, talking about politics, the American military bases, Subic and Clarke. Pauline sensed something in his dark, intense eyes. She saw that Ray was gulping his drink too fast. The caddie rocked rhythmically; rock, rock rock, calming himself down. He told her about history courses at a Manila college he had attended part time. Reading sharp, cynical writers, he said, he felt a fervent awakening, an insight into the past. His profile was like Rizal's, Pauline thought, mentally adding the national hero's Hapsburg chin. What an unusual and seductive country this was, their national monument a novel.

Later, Ray sat in front of the television, watching Trevino hit a perfect drive on the screen. She was surprised at how unreal the grass and flowers in California looked. As if someone had taken a cloth to each blade and petal and wiped it clean of the smog. Must be the camera. Filtered through the lens, only the grandeur came through—the lushness of the grass, the azure of the sky. It never looked that good when you were actually there.

◦◦◦

Back at their bungalow in Manila, she finished reading the newspaper in the lanai. The Peninsula Hotel advertised a Filipino feast coupled with Tinikling: a spectacular show. A feast for the senses. Eat sumptuous adobo and pansit while you watch exotic Filipinas in dazzling, traditional costumes. How wonderful, she thought, and walked towards the bedroom where Ray was taking a shower.

Behind the shower curtain, she saw her husband's soapy silhouette.

"Let's go out for dinner tonight. What do you say?"

"Okay Paulie, sounds fine to me."

"Hmm." The sound came out of her mouth but her eyes went fuzzy. Paulie. How long since he used that endearment. In the mirror, a blurred, soft face. That woman, Pauline thought, why she was still a girl playing grown up. Steam from Ray's hot shower made her freckled cleavage red. There was a time she used to tease him in the shower. With sudden energy, she opened the hot water faucet as if to wash her hands.

"Hey, Stop that!" Ray shouted, cursing at the gush of cold water from the shower. She shut the door, grinning to herself.

⁓

"The national dance of the Philippines," the hotel emcee announced. Accompanied by the roll of drums and tinkling sounds, dancers in festive costumes filled the limelight. Two men knelt on the floor of the stage, lifting, clapping poles of bamboo. The women moved gracefully, sticking thin ankles in and out, darting, agile movements, hypnotic to watch. Pauline loved the predictability of the rhythmic sound. Baronged men and women in butterfly sleeves offered trays of bibingka—sticky rice cooked in coconut milk. Pauline took one and felt the rice adhere to the roof of her mouth. Ray shook his head at the waiter, immersed in the show. Pauline wondered what he admired best about the dancers. They had proud, slender necks. Their glossy hair was pulled back in chignons. Perhaps he found their small waists erotic, alluring and fragile. A big man like him could crush these women like tender stalks.

Ray turned to her suddenly and said, "Why don't you join me next week when I go to Penang?"

Her eyes blinked fast, it happened when she was surprised.

"That would be fun. I'll read up so we won't miss the important sights."

⁓

Their only weekend in Malaysia and Ray was still lingering over the hotel breakfast. "Will you write to Mum or shall I?" she asked, bringing out the postcards, stamped and addressed. Ray's mother lived in Des Moines. Pauline knew she loved hearing from them, collecting postcards from afar. Des Moines was so dreary this time of year, all damp and miserable like a wet sock. Beyond a wall of windows was a view of rolling lawns; sunburned gardeners weeding flower beds. This is what it must have been like, Pauline thought, remembering historical photographs of Raffles, the famous hotel in Singapore. The book she had seen showed men staring grimly in the days of the Raj.

✑

Along with the tour group, they arrived at the snake temple in Penang. From the outside, the temple seemed ordinary. The light held you and you looked in, seeing only a small room, sleeping snakes. You had a choice to go in or stay out. Along with some of the others, Ray was being foolish, waiting to be photographed. The tour guide offered each of them a snake, wrapped it around Ray's neck like a scarf. "I think it's a bad idea. What misplaced trust," Pauline said. As if the essential nature of the thing would lie low so long, out there in the open, away from the intoxicating incense. Ray laughed and stood in front when the guide took the group photograph. What was he thinking, really feeling, stand-ing there like that? How annoying that he should take it all so lightly, as if she was the only novice there.

Inside the temple was a different matter. The snakes were small, black with brown patches, clumped here and there, dozing. The air smelled sickly sweet, the slimy green of tarnished incense burners blanketed by smoke, rising like humps from the gray stone floor. Thick with still shapes, the floor, the smoky space above, waited for a collective hiss. If you stood there long enough, Pauline thought, in that band of clear ground in the middle, the corners reached out and pulled, blue-black tentacles behind the fog. The movement of the smoke, curls thinning out, gave the impression of moving snakes, slithering darkness rushing to feet. It was like vertigo, the ground flying up to your head on the twelfth floor, pulling you down. You fell, a stillborn scream in your mouth, the plunge your only awareness for the moment.

Back at the hotel, Pauline soaked in the tub. Ray handed Pauline a glass of juice and undid the top button of his shirt, slid the knot of his tie. She saw red threads quiver in the whites of his eyes. "Better go easy on those," she said, pointing to his whiskey glass. The American orange juice smelled metallic, can on her tongue. The images of the day replayed in her head: the filthy streets the taxi had driven through, the ripe smell of strange foods and ditch water, the monotony of the land-scape, brown faces everywhere. So different from the words she had read. How real reality was. How it surprised.

༄

Weeks later, in Manila, on the day of their first office party, the cook was ill in bed. The driver, Torio, had brought his wife to help. Pauline was tucking ginger flowers into a big brass vase when screams emerged from the garden. Torio's girls. When the children arrived this morning with their mother, they smiled shyly at her. Drawing close to them, Pauline noticed their little dark heads were covered with nits. Wrapped in her robe, flower clippers in hand, she walked towards the pool.

Near the sprinkler, the girls danced and screamed, wearing only panties. The mother was frying shrimp wafers and chicharones on the barbecue. Torio leaned against the table under the santol tree, lining bamboo baskets with banana leaves. His trouser cuffs were rolled up. He had a straw hat on his head. Pauline saw that he talked with his wife as he worked. She watched them for a few minutes. As the girls slipped into sun-dresses she saw herself and Ray; a summer picnic, their daugh-ter Jesse, a toddler, sitting inside Mr Turtle, a baby pool in the yard. The memory stretched and tingled—she was aroused by poetry on her lap; Ray tracing the whorl of her ear with the tip of his tongue. She was reading Kubla Khan, preparing for a unit on poetry in her British Lit. class. Ray was dozing beside her on the blanket. He was recovering from a stomach virus he had brought back from his week in Ethiopia. He joked about meals from a communal plate, food that tasted like gym socks. She had stared at him shocked.

From the kitchen, Pauline grabbed a plate, toothpicks, olives, pineapple, cheese. She walked towards the children and held the plate out. "Please," she said, "take one." "Like this," she showed, stabbing a toothpick into an olive, then a cube of cheese. The girls bit into olives and made hideous faces. When the plate was empty, she hugged the girls, not caring that a louse could easily crawl up her arm or jump onto her head.

In the afternoon, a phone call from the States, from Mike and Sandra. Long distance calls made Pauline nervous. She talked faster than usual in a breathless voice. "We're having a luau this evening. Bamboo torches in the garden, the whole bit."

"We've mailed you a little something," Sandra said.

"Cranberry sauce," Mike interjected. "We thought you might find it difficult to get there."

"We're having lechon, roast pork. Like they have in Hawaii, a whole pig with an apple in its mouth," Pauline said. Mike and Sandra said that was nice.

"Do you need anything?" This was Sandra.

"Can't think of a thing," Pauline panted in reply. She heard Mike tell Ray about their trip to Palm Beach. They had played a few rounds of golf, he said. Sandra said thanks for the postcard from Penang. Before Pauline knew it, they were all wishing each other Happy Thanksgiving, saying the same thing, over and over.

After the party, she and Ray sat in the garden. The driver, Torio, and his wife were removing lawn chairs. On the pool were candles, floating in coconut husk cups. The fragrance of ylang ylang, the smell of rain hung in the air. "The typhoon season is coming," Torio said and wrinkled his nose towards the clouds.

"Are they very bad?" Pauline asked.

"Sometimes not so bad. Sometimes we have brownouts. No water. But this house has big pool . . . maybe many people come here for water."

Ray scowled in pain. "My back is killing me," he said, getting up, walking towards the house.

"I'll get the cream and tablets," Pauline said, watching him wince when he tried to turn his head.

In the bedroom, she saw that his face was flushed. He stiffened his arm as she unbuttoned a cuff. "This will help," she tried to soothe. She drew circles below the neck with the fleshy part of her thumbs. To play it safe, she had the medication from his doctor in Connecticut, a glass of water on the side table. She planned to make him swallow the tablets before they slept tonight.

"It's the hotel beds, damn soft pillows that are never the right height," he said. Pauline squeezed out gel from the tube. She rubbed it in with vigor this time.

"Stop it. It's starting to burn. I've had enough." Ray knelt on the bed making her drop her hands. Pauline recalled that his last check-up showed nothing. It had been attributed to tense muscles, stress. Pauline worried Ray's problem was psychological. He slept badly last night, kicking a restless leg.

"Damn fool," he had yelled at himself. "Fucking mind won't stop the replay of what happened at work. I can't seem to relax, unwind. Maybe I'm too old for this stuff." She had opened her eyes and reached for his hand. He looked so vulnerable. A child throwing a tantrum. He punched the pillow trying to shape it the way he wanted it, the way it sat in his mind.

"Stop worrying so much. Nothing can be done in the middle of the night. You'll be no good in the morning this way," she had said.

Perhaps they had been wrong. Coming here this way, so close to retirement. She should have remembered his passion for perfection. But it was supposed to be different, more fun this time. Why did he have to make a battle of things all the time? Earlier, when the guests arrived, he had put on quite a show. He charmed and flirted, dancing again and again with two or three of the local women. Pauline saw that he was having a good time. Without an audience, he displayed nothing of this public side for her, his wife.

༄

Sitting in the car, Pauline looked out at the veering jeepneys, their colorful streamers tied to antennas. Her right thumb absently stroked the knobby ridges of the hand-woven Ifugao fabric on the seat next to her. Braille against skin. Yesterday, the coffee party German hostess, now an almost friend, had dropped by for a visit. She suggested that Pauline go to her seamstress in Angela Arcade near the department store, Rustan's.

"Take your favorite wrap-around skirt. My seamstress Dolores, why, she'll make you one just like it," she had said, waving a hand suddenly, making Pauline blink.

Later, clearing their calamansi juice glasses, the maid said to her, "Ay nako, ma'm, my tiya Anching, she can make you same skirt for less than half-price. She is very good. Sayang, all that money, big waste ma'm. In Makati, everything too expensive." Pauline felt clever, she had discovered a bargain.

The driver, Torio, looked at her face in the rear view mirror.

"Quiapo very crowded near the market."

"Oh. Really?" She heard an edge of anxiety in her own voice. As they slowed down for a red light, she saw children, mostly boys, dart between cars. They were selling sampaguita strands—jasmine leis, cigarettes, chewing gum. Torio rolled down the window a couple of inches and whistled at one of the boys. As he pressed coins into palm, the boy turned to her in the back seat and fanned sticks of gum. She shook her head. Before the boy hurried away, a glob of saliva splattered on the ground. She patted the sweat on her nose with a folded tissue.

A few more minutes, having reached Quiapo, the car came to a stop. Torio shifted the gear to park and locked his wallet in the glove compartment. Hugging her pocketbook, she asked, "Why are we stopping? Is this the seamstress's house? Is this place safe?"

"This road okay," he said, pointing to a lane beyond. "That one very small, no good for big car. It's okay for me here. Okay for you. Walking is okay. No need to worry. I stay here nalang. Childrens coming and bothering car. Maybe scratch with stone. It's possible. Maybe Torio get mad."

Getting out of the car, he spoke in Tagalog to a woman carrying a baby. "You give him fifty centavos," Torio said to Pauline. "He will take you to Anching. Fifty centavos. That's okay." He repeated himself, as if she didn't understand. It was charming the way he confused gender when speaking English. Pauline had read that they used only the neuter in Tagalog.

The woman and the baby led the way and she followed in sandals, flimsy straps and all. A thin stream of soapy water raced down the side of the lane. Pauline's toes curled.

"My tiya," the woman announced, nodding at an old woman squatting and washing clothes under a gushing tap. Hearing the younger woman's voice, the huddled shape turned the bucket on the ground. Pauline attempted moving but it was too late, her feet were soaked. She cursed inwardly at the wetness on the road, her sandals, her lack of foresight.

She walked a few more steps. A man urinated into the gutter. Babes Stop Here the back of his T-shirt said. He turned his face and winked at her. Pauline tried to avert her eyes. But it was as if staring at him, she had frozen, turned to ice. She should not have hesitated. She should not have looked at him at all.

The sound of a child's insistent cry jolted her from her trance. Two other men had appeared from somewhere and they stood in the middle of the alley. They blocked her way ahead. She told herself to be calm, there were others about. As she walked, she looked sideways and past the men, focused on following the woman and baby ahead. Something she had written to her pregnant daughter Jesse in an old letter popped into her head. Pain belonged to the body, she had said, fear stemmed from the mind.

She walked closer to the men. They were hardly six feet away. "Hello ma'm! From USA?" one of them asked. The other one sang and played an invisible guitar, thrust out his pelvis, mouthing "I'm so lonely baby, I could die." A cluster of half-naked children watched and clapped. The man who had been urinating joined the others and they let her pass.

After they had walked for a while, the alley forked out ahead. There was a big crowd to one side. She noticed the woman leading the way walk straight ahead, pushing her way efficiently past spectators, swallowed by the crowd. Nearing the huddled circle, Pauline tried to squeeze through ahead but the lane was narrow, too many people shouting and waving fists at something going on in the middle. Men and women around her shoved and pushed, somebody stepped on her feet. What if she was trapped in a stampede? What a ridiculous, absurd thing to happen. Flattened like road kill. To dream of travel and end up smashed like a cartoon character.

Through gaps dividing tense shoulders, Pauline caught glimpses of the action. A black bird was scampering towards its opponent, coral comb rippling as it ran. There was a humming din of voices. The fight seemed to have taken over the people around her. They seemed in a neighborhood fiesta mood, some secret rage transferred into the tiny knife that flew again and again with the bird's leg. Only Pauline saw the cruelty, smelling the sourness of bird shit on the ground. She felt a slow nausea rise. Turning, she pushed her way out of the sweating bodies. Someone elbowed her chest. That feeling of being hemmed in a strange dream, she couldn't trust herself to find her voice. Her guide and the child appeared suddenly in front of her. The woman pushed and jostled and reached for her hand. She led the way to seamstress Anching's house.

"Where were you?" Pauline heard her own fear, her voice whine like a child's.

"Ma'm. Cockfight exciting no? Come inside, meet my tiya," the woman said.

"Who?" Pauline asked.

"Anching. Yes madam. Anching also my tia," the woman confirmed. Was it possible that most of the women in these shanty houses were related somehow? Perhaps it was a bond based on their common condition in life, a kinship which allowed them to enter each other's lives. "Don't worry ma'm. My tiya will do good job for you." The woman tilted her head to one side as she spoke. "You will be happy. We Filipinos, we are good at making happy, no?" Pauline paid the woman and saw the way she smiled.

In seamstress Anching's house, the odor of dried fish invaded everything in the room. There was an altar above the old sewing machine, Mary holding baby Jesus, wearing plastic flowers. Baskets of spools, fabric remnants in folded triangles littered the linoleum floor. Anching pointed to the makeshift changing room at the corner, instructed Pauline "Ma'm, wait there nalang." Minutes later, she entered, waving the curtains aside. "Magandang," she exclaimed, "That means beautiful.

The color is very nice." She wrapped the fabric around Pauline's slip, removing pins from a grimy cloth apple to mark the hem line. "Matching blouse?" she asked as she measured wrists for cuffs. Anching's eyes rested on the lacy cups of Pauline's underwire bra. "Imported ma'm? Sexy like bomba movie star." Pauline smiled and reached for her dress, facing the mirror this time. "You give deposit, fifty pesos now." Why that commanding tone? Anching reached out to adjust the twirl of Pauline's bra strap. Sandpaper fingers. She jerked back. Anching laughed and closed the plastic curtains that bordered the changing area.

Before Pauline could slip into her dress, a brown hand tugged at the curtains and parted them wide. In the mirror, a red-eyed man, tails of a bandanna framing his face like Arafat. Where was Anching? Who was this man? She suddenly recognized him as the same man she had seen urinating into the gutter. He took a step towards her; his face loomed over her shoulder in no time. The dress in her hand fell to the floor. She felt a heaviness, something stone-like spread in her chest. Anching's voice shouted at the man from somewhere, perhaps outside. He yelled something back. It all seemed to happen in slow motion, not nearly fast enough.

Pauline saw herself hunched over slightly, bra strap loose, a band over her arm. The unbearable smell of his sweat. She opened her mouth to scream but no sound came out. Something gushed, whirred, a strange disturbance in her ears. His dark eyes darted from her face to her breasts. In the mirror, she stared at the stain of her tan over her throat and neck. Finally, she managed a childish, whimpering sound. Behind her, the man bent down. She recalled the image of the altar in the room. Please. Dear God. He was standing with her wallet in his hand. Rummaging for something, he found a wad of pesos bound with a rubber band. "Anching say fifty, okay?" Pauline watched as he pocketed a wad of fifty single notes. Before closing the empty wallet, he noticed the photograph—Jesse and the baby. He looked at them and then at her. "Lola?" he pointed at her and laughed. "Anching my lola, granma," he muttered, tossing her wallet against the mirror. He picked up her dress and put it around her shoulders like a shawl. In the mirror she saw the starched linen dress gathered like a ruffle over her bra. Then he was gone. Only the smell of stale fish, his sweat, the curtain swaying to the gust of a table fan. She had not seen that framed picture on the wall above the mirror, Imelda Marcos in stiff organdy butterfly sleeves, mouth beginning to crack a knowing smile.

Out in the alley, there was only Torio. He walked towards her to tell her he had moved the car nearby. She saw that he was holding a book in his hands. Rizal's *Noli Me Tangere*. She remembered the title meant do not touch me.

"Everything okay?" he asked after they drove out of Quiapo. She found herself nodding into a crumpled tissue, fighting the nausea, a lemon Lifesaver spreading tartness in her mouth. There was a knot in her throat from the effort it took not to cry. Sweat was pooling at the base of her back.

"Ma'm, typhoon is coming. I hear it on the car radio." Torio turned up the volume. She heard the radio announcer suggest stocking up on candles, batteries, bottled drinks. This was followed by news about a ferry sinking off the China sea. Everyday, she thought, in countries she had never been or read about, there were people who suffered and survived.

ᴄᴏ

As the car turned into their driveway, she noticed Ray's car. In the kitchen, "Is he home so soon?" she asked.

The cook nodded and said, "Sir is lying down ma'm."

When Pauline opened the bedroom door, a small woman leered back. Two coarse and stiff hairs stuck out from a mole poised like a legume on her chin. Pauline noticed her teeth were shining and yellow in the dark of the room. The curtains were drawn to keep out the glare. The woman's toes squished the flesh along Ray's spine, the fuchsia of cheap nail polish popping like fake blood. "What the hell . . ." The cook was behind her in an instant. She lay a hand on Pauline's shoulder and drew her back.

"It's okay ma'm," the cook said. "She knows what to do. I phone her because sir is suffering."

Pauline barely whispered, "But she's . . ."

"Midget?" the cook asked. "But very good masseuse. Sir will be better soon, promise ma'm."

In the living room, Pauline gulped from a glass of gin. It burned all the way going down. Ray's eyes had been closed, his face serene. Why did he have to look like that? Her husband, a dancing midget on his back. Mike and Sandra had been right. Europe was one thing, but this. All those years together in the States, did she know all there was to Ray?

co

She came out of the house and stood under the carport. Studded on the bush beside her were ylang ylangs. The flowers were drooping and brown.

She did not remember how long it had been since she was standing there.

"My tiya," she heard the cook say to Torio, introducing the masseuse.

"He is small but looks very strong," Torio said.

The wind picked up in strength, hissing shrilly through trees, hurling a wave of dust. She could smell the moisture in the air, it would rain any minute now. Everyone began to move: the masseuse and Torio fetching bags, preparing to leave for home; the cook and maid running to get the clothes on the line. Ray appeared with a towel around his waist, raised his right hand, a visor to shield his eyes. Pauline heard the people around her, felt her eyes close as the dust swirled about her face. In her head, she saw Ray again, his fleshy, pink-skinned profile.

She was still in the carport after the others had left.

Ray was calling out to her from inside the house. She shivered slightly; the nausea had returned. At the club in Springfield, she watched herself step out of the cart. Ray stepped out too, rubbing the small of his back. She tilted their glasses of water, lots of ice, into the flower bed by the clubhouse. The water transformed into rain, dramatic and tropical, falling around her in Manila. Ray was calling her again from inside the house. His voice made her nausea rise. It moved snake-like through her body and heaved itself from her mouth.

Bee Mind Lotus Bud

WHAT IS IT? THIS LIFE? How to do it? Practice living? Under a towering cedar hedge at Avlokh High School, in the sunlight, I meditated at lunch recess. For a minute, when no thoughts floated in and around my brain, just blue-gold splotches moving behind eyelids, I relaxed completely. I played a game with myself. I would find the answer to my questions when I opened my eyes. I opened my eyes. On the ground in front of me, I saw ants hurrying up and down a sloping mound. Up and down they carried something too small for my eyes. They had no worries. Just that moment, stretching it by moving, living as best they knew how. I took a twig and broke up the mound. Now they were frantic, losing sense of direction. I, Bora, was one of them; studying in twelfth class. I was born in North Gunda province of Venoyo Island south of Cheju, the Sea of Japan to the east and the Yellow Sea to the west. How strange and small; me, the ants, everything. I was just an ant trying to figure out life. How to do it? Practice living in this world? How big the questions were.

During Physical Education, the drill master blew his whistle. As somebody kicked the soccer ball and it flew I imagined it to be me, Bora, soaring high, getting a better view of things. What did I see from up top?

This agility here on the ground, how meaningless, all sweaty and smelly. How to play hypocrite, pretend this was education of my kind? When the ball landed on my head and I rubbed the sore spot, my friends shouted "Bee mind." They meant I didn't concentrate, leapt from thought to thought like bees from flower to flower.

"Bee mind Bora, where were you? What's your problem? Fifty push ups there near the cedar hedge," the drill master yelled. I tried not to mind so much, because it was true, there was much dreaming, this droning in my head. I pushed myself up and down from the grass, roots and soil under my palms. I contemplated the lives of insects around me, those my eyes could not see. Such good company, no complaints from there. Just knowing they were there, like the skeletons of earthworms I pressed on the soil as I seesawed. I tried to make up a new riddle. If an earthworm is manly this end, feminine the other, which end do you face when you push up against them? Always, I told myself, the company of insects and plants, the lower form of life, the quiet and serene.

ᕲ

Wednesday morning was Watanabe San's art class. Watanabe San had told us she came to the island from Kyoto with her parents when she was young. Her hair swayed on her shoulders like strings of my favorite seaweed, her skin glowed like shiny persimmons. Sometimes, when she laid a fingertip on my shoulder guiding me through my work, her touch was live wire, lighting up tingly feeling whole length of my spine. I wanted to grab and kiss her hand, but then I wondered could I be electrocuted from too much pleasure? We looked out the window at a clump of bamboo trees. In black ink, we drew our outlines. Stiff stems, soldier leaves. Watanabe San was a small woman with an expressive face. She raised her eyebrows and peered into our sheets. Then she stood in front. "Art is not easy. Don't make copies, duplicates of stems and leaves. This time, don't use only eyes. Make your mind bamboo. Look. Pay attention. Then think. And dream."

Watanabe San moved next to me. I bent my head and erased an invisible dot in the middle of my sheet. The dot became a hole.

The next day, we were drawing again.

This time, we were outside. I had the sketch pad on my lap and I sat on the grass, away from the others. After typhoon Aija last week, a big tree had fallen at the edge of the woods, beyond the playground. I drew roots covered with mud, a frozen octopus bursting from the stem. Ferns sprouted here and there, insects and moss pressed and clung to the wood. For extra detail, hidden among the roots, a snake's head peeked out shyly.

When Watanabe San returned our drawings, she had drawn a small lotus bud in the bottom corner. Inside the bud, there were numbers— my best marks in art class.

Every day after class, she asked, "How is my lotus bud?" and then one day she gestured with her hand, come here. "Bora, promise me one thing," she said. "You must continue always with your art. Even after graduation next year." It was as if she knew me better than I knew myself. Under the towering cedar hedge in the school garden, I rocked back and forth, cradling my good part, lotus bud seed in my head. There it settled, lulled with each sound of my thud-thud heart. The lantern festival holiday weekend was before me, I tried not to think of my report card.

⌒

My parents died when I was only two. Skidding into a hairpin bend, they flew with bus wheels, diving into nirvana. Since then, I lived with grandfather and my sisters. But last month, he had resigned from his government job, decided to go to our ancestral village in North Gunda. My sisters, recently married and pregnant, lived in houses nearby.

The table was laid with my favorite foods: fried squid, sticky rice, tofu in garlic and chili sauce. Sunday lunch we all dined together: me, grandfather, my sisters and my new brothers-in-law. In the morning, I had watched grandfather pack useful things in trunks. While we ate, my new brothers-in-law, partners in a nuts and valves business, tried again and again to recruit me for a summer training job. All day long, they sat in an airless room, walls covered with shelves of nuts and bolts, counting metal pieces like tiny toys.

When we finished lunch, number one sister brought out an envelope. My report card lay on the table before us. Sister number two got up from her chair and came and stood by my side. She put her hand on my shoulder. I could smell her jasmine perfume called Queen of the Night. I wanted to pinch her plump cheeks but I could tell from her face that this was not the time. Number one sister looked as if she was going to cry. My marks were poor in all subjects except for art. The older brother-in-law, the one who swallowed his burps, smiled superciliously. The younger one farted and examined the ceiling, looking for hairline cracks. They suggested I go to their alma mater after graduation, a famous business polytechnic in the city. The college stressed team work and discipline. After graduation, their students soon found jobs. Grandfather banged his fist on the table and said, "Marks mean as much as a hollow gourd in real life. Let the boy go to the countryside monastery for a few days and think, gain merit by lighting a lantern at Ponchen Wat."

"Please," I said. "I want to do as grandfather says. I want to go to Ponchen Wat." I wanted to succeed on a different level—contemplate philosophy, float above reality, make drawings like mountain monks. After graduation, I pictured my classmates in their city college rooms, snake eyed from too much reading, minds chained to thick texts.

❧

At the train station, grandfather and I did not say much to each other. He was leaving in a few days for North Gunda. We felt too stirred up to share our thoughts. If one of us began a sentence, I thought, the other might break down. This way, instead of my saying good-bye to him, he was saying good-bye to me. I decided to climb into the compartment immediately, wave to grandfather from the window.

Inside the small, double occupancy, men only compartment, a monk sat on the lower berth, eating fish eyes. Glancing at the color of the bowl, I knew he belonged to the famous Ponchen Wat. Just the two of us. Soon I was settled on the upper berth, lying very still, waiting for the train to move. I could hear grandfather and the monk exchange greetings, clearly at first, then faintly, as the monk stepped outside to join grandfather on the platform. I turned my head and looked at them through the top band of window near my head. They seemed to be talking animatedly, waving arms about. I would later find out the monk had known my mother and grandmother; he was a fellow citizen from North Gunda.

Lying on the upper berth, I reminded myself grandfather always said sleep was a very good thing. He said that about the rains also. Grandfather said the rains announced something important. But now about sleep, I told myself. Sleep Bora ants sleep Bora sleep part of life is sleep. 12345678910 1. Sleep Bora 2. Ants sleep 3. Bora sleeps 4. Part of life is sleep. Sleep Bora sleep sleep sleep.

I slept.

An hour or so later, the train whistle entered screaming into my dreams. I opened my eyes and tried to understand where I was. From the lower berth came a voice, "Allow me to introduce myself. My name is Kimwa."

"What?" I looked down and saw a man in claret robes. "You are a monk?" Then I remembered, I had noticed this before.

"What do you think?"

"It appears to be so."

"But still, one wonders if that is the case?"

"I do not wish to offend."

"The just awake state is a holy state. One cannot deceive for a while yet. Truth is carried to your mouth from your dreams." I smiled weakly and realized I was still lying down, talking to him with my face over the metal bar that bordered my bed. Me, a high school student and he, a monk from Ponchen Wat. I jumped down from the upper berth and bowed before Kimwa. "I do not wish to offend."

"Think nothing of it." He adjusted his black rimmed spectacles and motioned with his hand for me to sit near. Then he spoke with fishy breath. "Difficult to hatch from family egg. Short climb from within but big stretch outside. Your name?"

"Bora. Born in North Gunda."

"Yes. Your grandfather mentioned it. Delighted to meet fellow citizen from North Gunda." A single fish eye sat at the bottom of his begging bowl. The wheels of the train went tuck a tuck tuck tuck a tuck tuck. I felt very relaxed sitting there with him, watching him read a book of Zen verses. I looked out the window at the scenery flying by.

"Bora, something you want to say to Kimwa?" At the sound of his voice, I turned around. He had put the book away, was looking at me with his black bean eyes. I sat there next to him and talked and talked. I told him everything: school, grandfather leaving, art class with Watanabe San, bee mind lotus bud condition in my head, business college, my sisters and brothers-in-law.

He looked out the window and stared at the sunset. The clouds dripped color like freshly cut watermelon; the tracks ran black and braided on the ground. As suddenly as before, when he had first introduced himself to me, Kimwa turned towards me and said, "the sun is bleeding, good time to meditate." I watched as he covered his face with a cream colored cloth and lay down.

"Why the cloth Kimwa?"

"To block the view, turn my eyes around, pull the answers out."

So that is how it feels to glide in and out of wisdom so effortlessly. What it must take to dance like him in that thin space, that pallid boundary between truth and illusion. His chest moved up and down in regular rhythm. Sleep or meditation? How educated the differences were.

At our station, a small group of monks came to receive Kimwa. A lot of nodding and bowing, chattering non-stop. Kimwa and I walked on the muddy street towards the monastery. Behind us were more monks. I was aware of the collective clip clop of wood sandals like the sound of horses trotting on a cobblestone street. A bird cried loudly somewhere above me. I noticed that Kimwa had been very quiet all this time, calculating something, drawing zeros in the air beside me. He had told me he worked as a detail monk in the treasurer's office, juggling the philosophical with the mundane.

"Kimwa, is it so very difficult to be a monk?"

"When you decide to be one, the decision would have to be considered carefully. But if you fail in the monastery you would be tossed out into the real world. If you prefer the mental and philosophical life, then Ponchen Wat might be the place for you. I will not discourage another from North Gunda."

❧

Away from home and school for the week, the setting of the monastery was a relief to me. I felt a great calm as I joined Kimwa in the main hall. To the farthest corner of the hall stood a giant image with an unfathomable smile. Behind the wooden altar was a silk scroll. The calligraphy painted on it appeared to be a poem of some sort.

> *Biting into a particle of dust,*
> *Pyong is crushed and flattened:*
> *Now the great yawn itself is full.*
> *It is cold on a winter's day;*
> *a single flake boasts of wetness.*
> *A marble child, riding a cat,*
> *disappears over the peaks.*

At the bottom of the scroll was the final sentence. "When the student wrote this, the master said to him: Now you lead and I follow. " What did it mean? As I circumambulated the image, the words began to haunt me. The monks lived a mystery, apart from the rest of us. I noticed their faces betrayed nothing as they greeted visitors and showed them around the compound. This world of wisdom and mystery was very appealing to me. Leap from the world, meet the true self, the poem said. I felt a surge of energy in my face, my feet, my body, my lotus bud head.

❧

As custom dictated, I chose a lantern for the evening lighting ceremony, requesting the monk at the booth to include the names of my grandfather, my parents, my sisters and brothers-in-law along with mine in the merit certificate. The monks had decorated the lanterns with crinkly paper for a festive effect. I lit the candle in mine and hoped it would not catch fire. If it did, the monk at the booth said, they would knock it down since adjoining ones might be ignited. This would be a bad omen. I was too big to call my parents for help but I must admit, I turned to them and begged for a sign. *Let the flame burn undisturbed, let this be my sign.*

Coming out of the main hall, I noticed two monks surrounded by lay people. "Who are they?" I asked a man nearby.

"Senior meditating monks," he replied.

Lay people bowed and folded their hands before these monks, offered them fragrant white flowers, plates of glutinous rice cakes and hard candy. The senior monks accepted these things without expression. They bowed back and gave away the plates. That was when I noticed their hands.

"What happened to their fingers?" I asked the man again.

"Burnt in penance," he whispered back.

Outside the compound, I spread my blanket under a pine tree. Through the gaps in the bamboo fence, I watched my lantern. *Let the flame burn undisturbed, let this be my sign.* The flame burned steadily in the windless night. I thanked my parents for I had learned the dead were sometimes alive.

~

The day before I left Ponchen Wat monastery, Kimwa and I met outside the treasurer's office. We walked towards a persimmon tree.

"Kimwa, remember what I said about the business polytechnic in the city? I don't belong there, I would like to try to be a student monk."

He was silent. His black rimmed spectacles slid down his nose; he wrinkled his brows. He drew eighths on his thigh with his right index finger as we walked. I smelled a fishy smell coming from his clothes. There was uneven stubble on his head. I watched as he shut the world out, chanting quietly to himself. I felt a surge of admiration for my new friend. He seemed truly wise. Aside from grandfather. But grandfather was moving far away. Kimwa finished praying and used the edge of his shawl to wipe his neck and head. I turned to him and said, "Help me explain to my sisters, Kimwa, you are also from North Gunda. Business college is not for the spiritually inclined. The world of my brothers-in-law, scheming profits for a living—that is for the absurd man. You alone understand the struggle in my heart." Kimwa raised his hand as if he'd heard enough. If I continued to feel this way, he said, I should visit again after the end of the school year, get permission to become a student monk.

☙

It has been five months since grandfather left for North Gunda. It was strange to live in number one sister's house and go back to Avlokh High, not see grandfather's face crumpled in sleep in the same room at night.

Last week of art class before examination period when I emptied my desk, Watanabe San smiled and asked, "How is my lotus bud today?" She gestured come here with her finger and gave me a book I could take home, pages filled with photos of paintings, passages describing lives of artists in faraway countries like France, Holland and Germany. I loved Watanabe San but I knew I had to say goodbye. There was no room for a woman in a monk's life. Late that night in my room, I saw that the book featured photos with marbled bodies the color of peeled radishes. I read about a Dutchman, Van Gogh, who, out of passion, offered a woman a gift of his ear. To behave like a mad man. Love was something terrible and wonderful to make a man feel like that. I was glad Watanabe San had promised to write to me in the monastery.

My calendar was marked till the last day of school, last Saturday of the month. I had written to grandfather about my plans to become a student monk. I had not yet spoken to my sisters or brothers-in-law. Ten more days before school ended, twenty more before I told them of my plan.

☙

My sisters were furious at first, saying I was too young for that kind of life. Far from the village in North Gunda, Grandfather came to my side. He wrote and said he was pleased to hear the rains had begun. It meant his grandson had discovered something important. Years before my birth in the village, he wrote, mother had prayed for a quiet son, a strong boy who would grow to understand the ways of the past. Grandfather said it was an honor and a privilege for the family, Bora the only boy, a spiritual potential at last.

Grandfather telephoned and spoke to my sisters. He assured them I'd be with the kitchen monks for three to five years. He explained about the long period of probation before I could be ordained.

In number one sister's garden outside, I rocked back and forth, cradling lotus bud in my mind. I imagined it stirred, burst out in bloom. All my life I'd been waiting for something like this to happen. What is it? What is this life? I'd been asking myself. "What is it?" I said now to the ants crawling in the garden. They buried themselves in the soil. "What it is?" I said to the birds in the birdhouse. They flew to the tree tops. "What is it?" I asked the neighbor's dog. He grinned and panted, grinned and panted, breathing hot mildew breath. Because of last night's rain, I saw earthworms everywhere, shimmying all around, wriggling designs at the foot of a tree. I stepped on one and watched it multiply. The earthworms—those lowly lives —taught resilience. I respected their wormy acts.

I heard my sisters cough. They joined me in the garden and shifted their weight from leg to leg. Then they grabbed their gurgling stomachs and pressed their lips to my eyes. All I could think of was my future life in the Ponchen Wat monastery, contemplating philosophy, floating above mundane reality. I pictured my friends in their city college rooms, snake eyed from too much reading, minds chained to thick texts.

⌇

I entered the mountains and became a student monk.

⌇

I joined Ponchen Wat, a humble novice eager for training. The pristine waters of Dhomle Bhap ran sinuously nearby. Persimmon orchards extended to the foot of the Great Blue Mountains. The rice fields to the east were bordered by long, horizontal vegetable patches. To the south stood granite slabs planted deep into the ground. They carried inscriptions containing the history of the Wat. The idyllic setting was a place of possibilities. I felt auspicious balls bounce pings in my gut. I thought about my classmates and tried to picture them with me here. No. They belonged in city colleges as I belonged here.

On the first day, I was given gray hand-me-down robes of a monk who died the previous week. Only the senior monks wore easy-care cotton/polyester. Beginners like me had to wear 100% cotton robes that needed to be starched and ironed. Kimwa told me how to prepare the starch by pressing rice through a cloth bag. I noticed my robes were heavily patched. When I pointed this out to him, he bowed and said I was indeed lucky. Later, as the weeks went by, I discovered that patches were like monastic muscles, a kind of status symbol. During free time, I saw some monks working with needles, adding squares of cloth to give the impression of tilled fields. I laughed inside glad I was free of such pride.

Kimwa took me to the kitchen compound where I would work. Novices like me slept in the annex off the great hall. My wooden pillow, cotton quilt, needle and primer of introspection were piled neatly on the shelf. The label below said postulant 5201. I looked at his wise-owl face and hesitated. "What is it?" he prodded.

"I'm no good with books. What if I fail?" I blurted. His face relaxed, he laughed out loud.

"We don't grade you here. Don't worry." I exhaled with relief; I felt my chest sag.

Afterward, Kimwa took me to the tank at the back of the Wat where I would wash in the morning. The wooden mallet to break the ice hung from a nail on the bark of the persimmon tree. Because of the different sleeping schedules of the various monks, sliding paper panels were used as partitions. Night sitting monks did not wish to oppress others by flaunting their dedication. That night, I could see the glow of a candle in the far corners as they sat up late into the night, traveling deep into themselves. I dreamed of myself as a senior monk, sitting up, meditating for days, my concentration so intense that I was lost for months.

During meal times, I observed silence like the rest. I learned to eat less, to swish and gulp the washing water that was poured into my bowl. I offered my waste water to the hungry ghosts in the fields. I learned that because of their small mouths, phantoms choked easily. I puffed up whenever Kimwa came to the kitchen and ate with us beginner monks. Here was a senior who liked me, he who dealt in infinities I didn't know about yet. Although ordained years before, Kimwa was the most unassuming monk I knew. I could see his dedication to his job was sublime. At mealtimes, he suddenly stopped chewing, put his spoon down, and began drawing numbers with his fingers in the air.

✧

As a novice monk, my beginning curriculum involved grueling physical labor. This work included one hundred and thirty prostrations each day, cleaning the latrines, working in the steaming kitchens and breaking my back in the fields. Mindless work was the best route to mindfulness training, the senior monks said. For beginners like us, monk Pyong, my stern regular teacher, taught that training began with watching.

"Walk in slow motion, not your normal pace. While engaged in walking, make sure your toes end at the same line as your nipples. Your awareness should be on the rise and fall of your knee, the heel and the foot. Observe how the heel lifts off, see how the toes brush the ground. While thus engaged, do not glance about with your bee mind."

Did he mean me when he said bee mind? I looked left and right to see if the other novices had noticed he meant me. They were looking down, concentrating.

Pyong continued. "It is courting fickleness to take in the pebble, the sharpness of its tip. This should not form an inherent part of your exercise. This is lust of the retina."

Through the following months, hours before sunrise, when I heard the bamboo clacker strike, I rose quickly and proceeded to complete my prostrations while we lined up outside the latrines. Most of the others chanted at this time. I preferred silence at that hour. First thing in the morning, I liked to smell the ground, feel my forehead on the grass or the cement floor. When I finished, I could hear my heart race and my head felt very clear.

In the kitchen, I helped to prepare rice, side dishes or soup. Even though this was not necessary, I worked with the rolling pin by my side. I knew that when cooking work was done, I had to memorize verses and more verses from the scriptures. I rolled impatience into kitchen rags as they lay flat and unyielding on the rocky slab.

Feeling particularly brave one day towards the end of the first quarter, I posed a question to Pyong. "You are lazy," he said, "You should learn to find your own way." Unable to fling a retort, I ran to the tank, pounding the mallet hard. The other monks thought such display dangerous. My beginner's curriculum was followed by intermediate courses that cracked the even more difficult realm of contemplation. I had to be certified fit to continue by Pyong.

It was during this difficult time that I met Kimwa. He listened patiently as I emptied the weight inside.

"Stop whining. Most monks take years to make. You want to throw tantrums like a child? Is this what you want them to see? Let Pyong and the others see your unique self rise."

I hung my head. All through that day, I pinched my thighs repeatedly. I imagined bee mind was a beard. That brambly thing, soon I'd find a way to shave it with a blade.

Standing in the middle of a row in the carrot patch, I adjusted the basket hanging from my back. Afternoons, out in the fields, the sunshine was strong, scorching everywhere with uniform strength. I bent and knotted carrot tops into a ponytail and pulled out firmly in one stroke. This way, the carrots came out whole. Then I twisted and tore the leaves, tossing the bunch into the basket Kimwa was wearing in front. He was doing the same, tossing leaves into front monk's basket. The carrots we collected in cloth bags that hung from our waists like kangaroo pouches. The monk behind sneezed two or three times. I turned and recognized Pyong, my teacher. It was a shock, seeing him in his striped shorts, skin like yellowed tracing paper, ribs, hollows moving in and out with every breath.

Pyong said to me, "It is high tide swallowing the beach sand, low tide making bigger beach. It is underwater sound, the sound you made before you had your tongue. What is this I am talking about? You know this?"

I gulped my saliva and heard the thud-thud of my heart.

"Divine sound?" I said softly.

Pyong guffawed and said, "Not divine sound, only Bora sound." He kicked me so hard my basket slipped.

Kimwa stopped working and turned towards Pyong. "When you pick carrots, pick carrots; when you teach, teach. Picking carrots and teaching means you're half picking carrots and half teaching. A monastery is no place for fractions." Kimwa walked over and gave Pyong a kick. Pyong bowed and laughed. Kimwa was my one true friend.

I loved harvest time best even though the work was relentless. The whole congregation participated with senior monks relating awe-inspiring mythological stories. Late in the afternoon, after we cleared the carrot patch, the Abbott, the kindest teacher of them all, told us about a story he heard from his teacher, the respected monk Kim-Son.

"One morning, as the sun was rising, a senior monk saw four of his disciples preparing for walking meditation. He caught a bird that had perched on the lowest branch of a tree. Gripping the fluttering bird in his hands, the monk said: "Postulants, utter one sound about this bird, show me a single act of wisdom and I will let it go." Clutching the tiny pink talons with his left hand, he demonstrated with a twist of his right thumb and forefinger that he planned to wring its neck.

My body became still as I listened to the rise and fall of my teacher's voice.

"The senior monk turned to the first student, the Abbott said. Tongue-tied and motionless, the young man stood with his eyes on the ground. The next postulant decided to act. He slipped out a needle from the hem line of his shawl and stabbed his thumb. He offered the teacher a drop of his blood, evidence of unflinching devotion, saying "monk blood is bird blood."

I realized I hadn't exhaled in a while. The Abbott's fish eyes clung to mine. He gestured; I averted my eyes.

"The senior monk spat on the ground. The third student, visibly nervous by now, ran inside. The senior monk was more than exasperated. The fourth postulant moved behind his teacher. He tickled the sides of the senior monk till he loosened his grip and let the bird fly. 'The bird knows to fly,' the student said. 'The sky does not end because of interfering monk. The sky is there so birds can fly.' The student monk bowed. He was glad to hear his teacher, the senior monk laugh and clap his hands."

I had never heard such a story. I tossed and caught carrots in mid-air. The Abbott had looked me in the eye all through the last part. Perhaps he had singled me out. Later that day, I received a letter from Watanabe San. She would remember me always, she said, her favorite pupil who made teaching worthwhile. Inside the letter were art cards, drawings of pine trees and rocks made by mountain monks. "These are for you Bora," she wrote in delicate handwriting, "For inspiration if you like." I touched the middle of my forehead. Lotus bud was there, tender and alive.

〜

I had spent hours in the kitchen making kimchi, pickled cabbage and turnips. I came out of the kitchen and stood with my drawing pad under a persimmon tree. One or two of the other novices also came out and stood under a neighboring tree. They were talking about the monks who had been ordained last week. Everybody had observed the change in them. Their bearing, their faces, even the way they walked was different, more still somehow. They had new begging bowls and easy-care robes. I could hardly wait my turn.

I noticed Kimwa spent a lot of time in the company of succentor Song-Sen. I asked him about his friend. Kimwa told me Song-Sen, like Howdah Two before him, (who had last month gone the great white lotus way) was the Wat's tofu delivery man. In the morning hours before noon, snowy slabs were carried in a cart attached to a bicycle. When the brakes began to fail, Song-Sen valiantly screeched to a halt by hugging trees and lamp-posts, whichever was around. Kimwa noticed the bloody state of his face one day and found him out. The bicycle was sold but there wasn't enough to buy a new one. Song-Sen had to get up earlier than before to make the slow trudge with a limping buffalo. The job now took twice as long.

I nodded my head slowly making lotus bud dance.

All this time, Kimwa explained, postulant Song-Sen stayed resilient, never stooping to utter a word of complaint. It was months later before the village store owner heard about the Wat's predicament and supplied a new bicycle. Impressed with Song-Sen's behavior, Kimwa wrote a letter of recommendation to the Abbott requesting advancement of his ordination. I was speechless for a while. If they were impressed so easily, I had a good chance. If it were me, I'd have pulled the wagon to the village myself, straining muscles taut, providing fuel for the job.

༄

Sunday mornings began with a serious talk. The message was hidden in a riddle for us to unwrap. It meant concentrating on a single verse continuously and without distraction. We had to empty our minds of weed-like thoughts. I worked hard trying to push myself inside. I felt an auspiciousness surge, the way I'd felt the first day.

The last Sunday of the month, the Abbott began: "Sex is life. But is life sex? The paw is the dog, the dog is the paw. If one has to bark, bark at the mind. Listen closely. Leave that thought behind. No mind, no thought, what is left? Do you see this?"

I sat there flummoxed. The senior monks shifted in their sitting positions. Others straightened their spines, made their eyes blink. I concentrated hard, tried to crack the riddle. I had to become daring, as courageous as one who yanks the tail of a running panther or seizes the feathers off a swooping hawk. I remembered the penetrating eyes of the Abbott, his startling intensity, as I clung to the riddle late into the night. Why this bee mind? What is it? This life? How to do it?

I had to go at the riddle alone, think myself the horn of a rhinoceros. I remembered important words from Watanabe San's letter, the one where she said she admired monks, specially young monks. Sweet madness of lovers, she called it, the thing that made them curl and look inside.

⌒

Then came the period before the meditation retreat, that lasted many days and nights. This time of year, the late senior succentor, I heard from the others in the kitchen, was usually very much occupied. This year, of course, since he had gone the great white lotus way, there was Song-Sen, doubling as chief succentor and tofu delivery man. He sent for me and said he had been observing me closely. I bowed feeling excited at the thought of being asked to meditate in the main hall. Before he could speak, I blurted,

"Please, though I am only a postulant, can I join the meditating monks?"

"I need you to be one of the tea-boys during the retreat. Can you do that?" Song-Sen asked. Song-Sen outlined the nature of my duties. "If you are not interested, then, of course . . ."

"I am . . . I am here to serve in any capacity," I said. I knew they considered me a novice drawing monk, but I would impress them by my willingness, my humbleness.

All through the retreat, I remembered stories I had heard in the kitchen from the other novices. I remembered hearing about monks who lived like hermits in the mountains barely subsisting on powdered rice and pine needles. Others, I was told, intent on standing meditation, lifted arms over heads for days, folded palms through the night, tied their elbows behind their backs. There was a story of a monk who stood on one leg till the muscles of the other atrophied from disuse. Total awareness, he claimed, was the *summum bonum* of his existence. Monks and artists, same beauty! What it took to behave like a mad man.

Most monks who participated meditated continuously stopping only to go to the toilet or eat. I was only a tea-boy and I was walking around in a daze, confused, dreaming of something else. Lotus bud burrowed deeper in my head. Sweet madness of lovers, I remembered, the thing

139

that made them curl and look inside.

The poison from bee mind dripped through the hours brimming late on the third day. Tripping with the tray as I made the rounds, I fell, cow-like, through the partitions of rice paper panels behind which the Abbott sat. I dared not meet the Abbott's face, I could feel fish eyes blaze and roll, an elephant in full rut. All I had courted and yearned for was the life of a simple monk. Propping up the battered partition, I fled the hall.

Kimwa had said that he always found the experience of the retreat rejuvenating in a strange way. He had discovered how to court concentration, make the mind bend in obedience. Other novices stopped speaking when I approached. Were they afraid I'd jinx things somehow? I wept repeatedly in the latrine. The dark hole gaped mirroring the chasm inside.

All of us postulants noticed the look of esteem given to the meditating monks by lay members when they came with their offerings of fruits and flowers towards the end of the retreat. Novices like me were never noticed. Looking gaunt and happy, the meditating monks broke the retreat with a special meal of glutinous rice cakes and hard candy.

The Abbott sent for me. He had noticed that even as a tea-boy, I needed more practice. Song-Sen also chided me and said I should try harder the following year. He prescribed thorough revision of doctrinal verses from the handbook for the following months."Pierce through your daily mind," the Abbott warned, "grab the core of your big mind," voice indifferent, elephant eyes looking out the window as he spoke.

Dismissed, I ran to my friend, the mallet hanging on the tree. It was spring, the water mocked—liquid—dancing with each touch of the wind.

Through the following weeks, I couldn't shake the nauseous feeling that Pyong was waiting and watching, ready to pounce. Kimwa spoke to me patiently as always, "Most monks take years to make, " he said. "You're throwing tantrums like a child. Is this what you want them to see? Let Pyong see your unique self rise."

The shame of it. He had to remind me again this way. I observed a period of silence for the next three days. I played back scenes in my head, my behavior in the past.

Kimwa was wise. How hard it was to separate me from bee mind. The struggle, this tug of war; lotus bud, bee mind, time had come for me to grow up.

My sisters sent letters full of concern, it seemed their farting, burping husbands had connections everywhere. It was more than I could bear. I pleaded with Kimwa. Turbulence like mine had to be quelled with force, this I finally figured out.

I carried a portrait of my parents in my knapsack. I stared into knowing faces, calling yet again. My gentle mother came to me in a dream, knocking at the back of my head. She rapped her knuckles hard and said "Is the coconut empty? Is the coconut a full bladder, only water inside?" Lotus bud revived and rattled as mother tapped with a spoon. "Antidote," she called it, "potent against poison of bee mind." I watched fascinated as lotus bud opened his mouth, pink petals flaming marigold, a mallet around his stretching neck. Lotus bud and I kissed mother's tiny feet with respect. My parents had again shown the dead were no less than the alive.

Sweet Watanabe San. At last I knew how to make the madness come to me, the thing that will help me curl and look inside.

౼

Late this evening, Kimwa and I met at the small shrine. Privacy was assured since this was where we confessed and recited our personal prayers. Kimwa produced a piece of cord from a knot in his shawl. He tied my wrist with it tightly. This helped calm my sensitive nerves. With the edge of his shawl, he wiped his forehead. He was sweating profusely. "Kimwa, I trust you. You are my true friend," I assured.

He unfolded a bit of burlap cloth and lit the candle before the image in the shrine. Both of us made obeisance and prayed reciting the evening incantation in our minds.

When we opened our eyes and lifted our heads, the candle was burning that last burn in which the flame wears a halo of blue. I watched the golden center, an upturned drop swaying in the middle, humming.

141

The cloth was now ready. Kimwa lifted it and placed it gently around my forefinger. A corner of the material stuck out like a tail in the place of a wick. He lit the tail and began chanting. He motioned for me to join. We chanted feverishly as my finger turned into a flaming torch. To keep the mind focused, I chanted loudly, almost shouting the words, my eyes tightly shut. I felt lotus bud rise, pushing through my skull.

I was aware that some of the senior monks would be critical of such ostentation. I felt no remorse about this. From them I learned that one finds his own method. Mine had splattered bee blood.

The other postulants and lay members would see the cavity when I gestured by folding my hands. It also helped that I waved my hand expressively while speaking, an old habit of mine. I had felt practically nothing, I tried repeating to myself. The throbbing in my hand continued like stubborn staccato beats. Suddenly I remembered that tomorrow was kimch'i making day. Would the chili paste and brine water make the stump burn? Or would it help speed the healing?

Lying on my quilt at night, I played a game with myself. What is it Lotus Bud? This life? This pain? How to do it? Practice living? Come talk, come tell.

I will find the answer to my questions before I close my eyes. An everlasting shot of pain, a terrible roundness, whole and full, lifted me outside myself. Elastic, I zoomed into that dirt speck on the wall, traveling and still by turns. I sat inside the moment. This life. This moment. That's what it was. Pain. Joy. A single moment. That was all.

Matsutake

THIS IS THE HINAYANA way: *Seek the watcher. Clap in your mind and call.* Words from my boyhood past, now a daily prayer. I am kneeling on the Oregon ground, feeling the coolness of the soil through the cloth of my pants. In my mind, a part of me sees my palms together, makes a deep *wai* to the forest, the trees. Gripped in my right hand is a checkered towel, wrapping the torn sheath of my favorite mushroom knife. The tip juts out silver, a nib in the morning light. I wish only to love and be loved, live a simple life.

A shrill whistle flies into my ears. Booted feet crunch leaves behind me; a voice suddenly swears, "Goddamn brownie. Filthy bastard." How many of them? Two? Three? I turn around slowly, straightening myself. A bulky pinkness moves close to me. I notice a bird tattoo on his chest, wings spread as he inhales, swells his chest. He kicks and topples my plastic bin of matsutakes on the forest floor.

"Please don't bruise or trample them," I want to say. But at that moment, I feel eyes clinging to the back of my neck. My right hand opens, the towel and sheath fall from my hand. They slip easily, without sound. I smell sour beer smell. My knees bend again, I squat child-like on the ground. The men make kissing noises, following comes rude laughter.

"We heard a group of you were grilling frogs last night. Grilling frogs! We want you fucking pigs out of here, understand?" I look up and see the man in front clenching his teeth when he speaks, jerking his head to the side showing me the way out. I am only half-listening. I am thinking his American arms are the size of my thighs. The second man is in my view. He has baby porcupine hair. I see a vest, a scar like a fat worm curled on the mound of his arm.

I close my eyes and speak silently to myself. My heart is waving in my ears. I tell it straighten out. "Sisouphan," I say to myself, "hold your breath and make your body wooden." These men in Oregon, they see nothing on my face. My mind stills my tonuge. Silence adds no trouble. Bullies are ciphers, bamboo pulp in the head. Remember what the monk said: *Watch for the watcher, clap in your mind and call.* It is only proper, nothing like a miracle when they drop their hands to their sides. My mouth takes little sips of air, greedy like a fish.

"I suggest you and your friends leave fast," the tattooed man hisses, snapping his fingers, turning to leave. Porcupine Hair spits out something he's chewing, scratches his groin, baseball style.

જ

When I wake, the sun has traveled a quarter of an arc. I fell down from shock, I think. I try to sit. I see nothing for a moment, not the forest, not the sky. I hear only the birds in the trees. My eyesight comes back slowly, a sheet of charcoal pierced with vague shadows, dancing fuzzy lights. The blood is sticky at the back of my head. A knotted tree root behind me bulges slightly red. I wonder if I hit my head right there.

Looking at the treetops, I press the back of my head with my folded towel. So that is the bigger plan. Make a man stop and think for a day. Perhaps then he's all right, maybe even good for a while. Sitting there on the forest floor, a part of me watches Sisouphan bring his hands together, make a deep *wai* to the forest, the trees.

To live quietly, working with my plants. Chant this in your head. Sisouphan is mostly safe in America. No hunger clawing in the stomach, on the way to becoming an educated man. Detach yourself from everything. Didn't the monk's prayer teach you that? Chant this in your head. Wipe away this sweaty anger; peek into your ugly part. What is out there in this other Sisouphan? Nothing, I tell you. Trouble comes often, even in America, don't you know this about life? But Sisouphan likes to watch himself. Pendulum mind swaying this way and that.

"Remember," I tell myself, "you are the son of a Laotian soldier who fought bravely, flying as a backseater for American pilots over the Plain of Jars." Though I have little memory of my father, I know he gave me this life. Before I left for America, that unknown place, mother said, "Sisouphan, my son, stay strong in your head. This is what you have." The chemicals from the yellow rain dissolve her body, making her an old woman. Her speech comes out in hoarse whispers, spluttering out of the raw crater that widens in her mouth.

Traveling to the past in my head helps a little because I take myself to the Ban Vinai refugee camp in Thailand, where I learned to gain strength. Chief guard is a bully, grabbing and pinching boys. There is no drinking water, no lights at night. All of us refugee children have illness, diarrhea. We sprout sores on our faces that attract black flies. If chief guard approaches me, I think, Sisouphan will be ready. I make myself into a box, hard and metal-like. This metal sends a numbing signal right into my brain. I mold the box to fit the contour of my skin, covering flesh and bones, flowing over blood. The method is effective and secret, nobody finds out, not even the clever boys in the camp, Nong and Moua. The idea is to leap into the box while pointy nails of hunger clutch and dig, clutch and dig. Deep in my stomach, the scratches become a background fact. Like the beating of my boyish heart.

My mother is heaving in the muddy corner; she vomits all the time. "See, Mama, that girl playing pretend marbles with pebbles, standing there near my friends Nong and Moua? She will be my wife." From the corner of the hut, Mama gives me a smile. I look at Mama, then at Xana. She is drawing fans with her foot like I had shown her, pressing her foot in the mud and turning it sharply to the right.

Awake in the dark, I hear the scurrying of rats, see their shiny slit eyes. There is a big one that makes an ugly chomping sound. I close my eyes very tight and say the prayer to myself. If I look up at the rats or stare at Mama's huddled and shaking back, I might be afraid. To help Mama who is sick and weak, I must try to be brave. The thing is, I don't know how to be brave. *Remember the Hinayana way. Bring here the watching self, push back the other selves. Clap in your mind and call.*

When I travel farther back into the past, I am a little boy in Laos. I feel the priest whispering holy words in my ear, his breath blowing hot. So many families seeking blessings, praying to stay alive. My country is turning into a giant pit. Too many of the people I love are gone. The sky rains bombis torching humans and animals alike. I pray also, wanting to escape death. I dream of love, Papa's fingers clasping mine; please give this child a life.

I am ten years old and scared, moving on a raft, carried by the force of the Mekong. Clinging to my mother's side, I hear the words of her prayer, the one she learned from the monk in Luang Prabang. I do not want to leave the purple mountains of my home behind. What is to become of us? While she prays in muffled gasps, my mother rubs my scalp with her palm.

Here in Ban Vinai refugee camp in Thailand, I miss Papa. What did he look like? His face fades sometimes. The nails in my middle clutch and tear. I spot a pigeon, aim a pebble with a sweaty palm. Shut the box quickly. Don't cry. Aim. Throw. If Sisouphan is slow, Mama dies, you die.

I hear myself whisper, "I am not ready to die."

Many evenings, mother and I eat the bodies of birds.

୶

Now in America, this is the plan. Work quietly in the forest in Oregon and do garden work in California. Pray and chant this in your head. Sisouphan is mostly safe in the present. No hunger clawing in the stomach, on the way to becoming an educated man.

I wish only to love and be loved, live a simple life. That was what I was thinking as I waved to Xana from the parking lot of the Pagoda, the restaurant in Redondo Beach, California, where I worked sometimes.

The sun was shining, making everything seem all right. Xana waved back, tells me, "Wait." I was thinking she will someday be my lovely wife. But I was not a clever man with words so the thought went unsaid. Xana knew of this shortcoming so she spoke for me. Small, wifely gestures. Like this leafy packet of fish paste which I slipped into my brown paper lunch bag.

The old red pickup rattles past my other place of work, the San Remos apartment buildings on South Catalina Avenue. Many times, I paint and varnish empty rooms there. In the foyer of the front building, the Super and I stick mirror tiles with veins of smoke so the passageway looks doubly large. In the open back of the truck, I hear the wind dance in my ears. I curl myself and close my eyes.

Monday to Saturday, Nong and Moua ride in this van. They cut grass. When I need the work, I go with them. We come up with a good routine. Nong mows the grass, Moua uses the edge tool, I rake and bag the clippings. Because Mrs Penn, our best customer, told them I have a special eye, I sometimes trim hedges, shape dwarf and big trees to let in the light. Watching me cut her key lime tree in the blue and white Chinese container, Mrs Penn told Nong and Moua about my special gift. I cropped the tree first in my head, she said, stepping back from reality to see the effect. "Sisouphan's hands move so gracefully. See how he follows the branch's natural tendencies." Moua nodded as if he understood, but I saw that he wrinkled his eyebrows. He gets only the gist of things when customers speak. His English is still basic. Nong knows even less: yes and no, some bad words, names of things to eat, numbers to count dollar notes.

Nong and Moua tell me they understand important things. "We know how to run a business, look out for ourselves, put money in our pockets—this is the way to respect." They believe I should learn these too. At first, I do not say a word. Then I tell them about my prayer; my wish for nothing material but everything for a full, inner life. Nong and Moua say "Sisouphan, you, this philosophy, we do not understand."

One summer afternoon, watching me yank weeds in her backyard, Mrs Penn calls out, "Seeesoufan." Moua stops and lights a cigarette. I tell him the edge tool in his hand is a moody machine. It spits smoke like he is shaving stones, not spiky blades of grass.

"Seeesoufan," Nong says and points to where she waits, under the big, guava- colored umbrella. She is holding a clay pot of phalaenopsis, bottom leaves splotched yellow and brown. Her voice is stricken like the plant.

"Do you know about orchids? What's wrong with this? It was just fine when I bought it. I water it everyday. Isn't that enough?" Poor plant. She wants it to live a soft, cushiony life. It needs humid air going round in circles, not water all the time.

"Charcoal pieces, lava rock, "I say, pointing to the bottom of the pot. She leads me into the kitchen, pulling a bag from the cupboard under the sink.

"How many?" she asks. I take the bag, re-pot the orchid right there, shaking sticky soil which clings to the roots. Mrs Penn brings out a vacuum that sucks up the mud from the floor. Like the inside of a shell, her kitchen is milky white again. I see a kettle with a border of baby ducks on the stove, copper pots and pans dangling from the ceiling, brass handles pointing up. On the table where she eats, a glass bowl like a bubble, grape bunches climbing out. Through the window, I can tell Nong and Moua are almost finished outside.

"Since you're here, let me ask you about my other plants." She goes into her bedroom. I follow. There is a giant plastic water bed, folded sheets and pillowcases piled in a corner, waiting to be stretched out. I do not know where to look. I step over the garden hose snaking water from the bathroom faucet to a hole in the bed. Mrs Penn points to the plants on a corner table. The wooden surface is covered with a lacy cloth, photos of children with yellow hair. What it must be to live like this? I try to picture Xana and myself in Mrs Penn's room. Would we drown, like her plants, sleeping on such a bed?

I bring the orchid and other plants to the bathroom where there is much sunlight. "They will like it here," I say, "Don't open the window after you take baths." The wallpaper is scattered with starfish. She wants me to come here for the next few weeks when she is away to look after her plants. The key will be in the house across the way, the one with agapanthus beds.

"Could you come in and take a look on Tuesday?" I nod my head.

That morning at the restaurant, when I look at Xana, I see that she is busy, concentrating on the smoking wok. She cups the salt in the middle of her palm, curving the sides like a curled leaf. I like to watch the way she cooks, intuitively gauging the taste by the weight of heaping condiments in her hand. *Con-di-ments:* a word I learned in my last week of GED English class. The teacher said to use our vocabulary words in sentences when we talk.

I forget to close my mouth when I see Xana cut big white onions very, very fast. It is wonderful to see, the way she has of slicing them so fine, making believe she's doing it without lifting the blade of the knife. She senses I'm watching and stops for a second. I can tell she is deciding whether or not to look up. When she looks up, she will act surprised to find me staring, hoping for her shy smile. But she does not look up. This is on purpose, I feel. Still a young one, heart full of games. My eyes rest on the plates she prepares. She arranges the food American style— mounds of colored rice, stewed meat and sauce bordered by green lettuce, orange slices, parsley on one side.

Xana looks up, shrugs her shoulders and says to me "It is what they like and expect." Such a clever woman, who enters easily into my thoughts. I smile and nod my head wildly making her laugh hard. She is holding the knife across her face to hide the gap between her teeth. I want to run to her and say, "Careful, careful, Xana, my future wife. Feel this love, you are so loved, this sweet-simple life between us." But I don't say anything, I stand and stand. Sisouphan the bamboo stem. Cockroach whiskers, I say to myself, leech skin and snake eyes. When are you going to open your mouth, pull the words from inside? I see that the steam from the cooking has made her face shiny. Two bits of her hair, the sides she has cut short, fall over her cheeks, reaching the same level as her lips. Her face is framed nicely by these raven wings.

I remember the day I got my GED. I cycle home from evening school, rushing to Xana. She is in the kitchen of the Pagoda, like always, chopping onions. "Look," I said loudly, surprising myself, waving my certificate. Staring at the paper, she almost cut herself.

"Sisouphan! Sisouphan! This is good, very good. We must do a *baci*, go to the temple. Now you find a better job. This washing dishes, wiping tables, not for you." I laugh at her chattering excitement, remind her that I have studying left.

"Better job after community college courses," I say. She nods and says she knows, Nong and Moua already told her about the application for a scholarship. Mrs Penn wrote El Camino college, a letter to push me in. I watch Xana's hand stir spicy sauce in a pot. As she steps back from the burping liquid, I step back, too. I am thinking Sisouphan will show Nong and Moua there are many ways. Learning. Tenderness. These are the seeds to grow in a man.

I park my bike in the half moon driveway and let myself into Mrs Penn's house. I go to the backyard and wait for Xana while the plants are soaking in the tub. The sun is making me sleepy. I lie under a eucalyptus tree making pictures balloon out in my head. *Sisouphan has slipped a lychee into Xana's mouth before asking her to be his wife. She nods yes and I grab her hands. I kiss her neck, the part where she smells like colored rice. Her skin has that special softness found only in a wife. Because we are soon to be American husband and wife, Sisouphan rents roller blades. He and she slide side by side in pretty Laotian dress. Xana is laughing like five-day-old bird of paradise. By the sea in California, this lonely place, I am suddenly happy. I wished to be loved, I am loved; living this simple life.*

This laughing wife and I, we buy a giant water bed that spreads and spreads. Nights I fall asleep, lulled by ocean sounds. Xana makes little waves as she turns again and again to embrace Sisouphan. Together we rock the nights away, this way and that, like babies crouched in a cradle. The bedroom walls are rounding out, carrying us away, depositing us in some faraway place. It runs out of me, this feeling like mountain stream water. To think that Sisouphan has thrown away the pain of his past life.

In the alley outside the kitchen of the Pagoda, when news from my scholarship letter had been squealed over and shared, I blurted out my wish to Xana, asking her to be mine. Xana looked away and said softly, "so soon, it seems so soon . . ."

"Xana, this is me, remember? I promised a five-year-old girl in Ban Vinai." Her fingers played the chain on her neck, looping it round and round, then letting go, before starting up. It was making me bubble up; I wanted to pluck and toss the thing aside.

"I'm tired of the past, Sisouphan. We'll always be friends, let it be that way. I want to forget those children in the camp. So many of us, crouching inside . . ." This was not the girl making brown-red fans, pressing her foot to the mud like I had shown her and turning it sharply to the right.

Inside the restaurant, Xana began to chop onions very, very fast. I snatched and pocketed the scholarship letter from the plate near her hands. I wanted to clip those drooping wings of her hair. She did not want me? To be loved by me? Live that beautiful life? I said "You knew all along. You knew how I felt. I only want to love and be loved, live a simple life."

Xana chopped and chopped, refusing to look up.

"Please understand Sisouphan. I do not feel this thing like you. Nong and Moua, them I understand. You? Where did you go? When did we lose you? What is that simple life?" I have seen her in the alley, playing giggle and pout with Nong and Moua. Now she played coy with me,"Sisouphan you, this philosophy, I do not understand." She wanted words. I offered none, standing and standing. Sisouphan the bamboo stem. Cockroach whiskers, I called myself, leech skin and snake eyes. "I am here," I wanted to say, "nowhere else you see. Breathing in and out before you, living inside out. That is the simple life. Touch my thoughts, Xana, this part of me, my nose, my eyes, my face itself."

Her eyes watered, wetting palm sugar-colored cheeks.

Grow up, I told myself, it could be onion, not you, that is making her cry. I closed the kitchen door behind me. Less Sisouphan, this small size; such a lonely place, this California, America; no country on earth for a pure man and wife.

~

I wake as the sky shifts color, peeling from the inky skin of a plum to honey flesh inside. Like always, I have opened my eyes before Nong and Moua. A carton with my things stands next to my bed. Today I move to a room in Torrance so I can cycle to El Camino college. Weekends, I plan to work with Nong and Moua, maybe wash dishes at the Pagoda. In the carton near me are my college texts, covers touching. Like two skins. The old black and white photographs with scalloped edges are tucked into journals. One, a wedding photograph, shows my mother and father in traditional Laotian dress. The other photograph, taken in Ban Vinai, shows my mother, a blurred vision of her former self. Next to her, me, Sisouphan, face marred by sores, the face of a man on a child. There is nothing left to do except carry that smooth, sore-free face out of the apartment for the last time.

I cycle slowly, very very slowly, away from Mrs Penn's house. Automatic sprinklers are hissing on her lawn. Underneath the water, I hear the silence. But above, where I ride, my mind is loud. A simple life is a difficult thing, it seems. To want this and that, want and want again. Why want to love and be loved, live a simple life?

Watch for the watcher; clap in your mind and call.

Praying helps my mind zoom into what I see: Mrs Penn's black cat sitting on the window sill, opals for eyes, opals split with black lines in the middle. Sisouphan cannot stop himself, he flies, opens up the black slits, turns around, watches himself cycling in Redondo Beach, California. To pull from inside while flying, love without loving, live un-seen, carry this quiet part about. That, that is the only way to survive.

༄

Here on the Oregon forest floor, Sisouphan the mushroom picker is cer-tainly a braver man, stooping to collect the matsutake. I see that my bin is filling up with other mushrooms. Not as many matsutake as I'd like. I place the mushrooms neatly in my bin, brushing off soil and pine nee-dles. There is always the afternoon, the day is only half done. A simple life is not a difficult thing. See Sisouphan here, living inside out. Kind and gentle, breathing in and out.

I hear scraping footsteps, twigs crunching behind me. My fingers tense around the handle of my knife. Only a diligent forest guard, trekking through the paths of the woods, checking licenses. I put down my bin and stick my hand in my pant's pocket. I feel the reassuring paper. My license is here, I am safe. I continue walking, looking past trees.

To live quietly, stop this pendulum mind swaying, that is the bigger plan.

Insects are injecting the skin on my face and neck. I try to make measured movements, concentrating on my steps. No forest guard in sight. Scampering squirrels all over the place, tails raised and curled as if they plan to lean back and rest. We stand still for a minute before we move, squirrels clutching nutshells between their hands, Sisouphan carrying a bin of mushrooms.

All the way to Oregon from California, I saw that Nong and Moua, my traveling companions, had lost their faith. Though young and strong, they wear guns against their chests. They say I am foolish and do not understand. "What is to understand?" I ask. They do not believe in prayers, they say, fighting to survive is prayer enough.

How then shall I speak to my friends, Nong and Moua, when we ride back to California? How to explain that I sometimes enter a place within myself, this quiet? "It is a nothing place, really, dark and light," I might say, wishing to tell them what it feels like. When I am there at the entrance, I am the only one alive. I am so deep inside the hole that the world is a comforting black. I begin to disappear, lose myself. For me, this is the very best part. Where I was before, not a trace remains, the space my body occupied is magically sewn up. Now when I move, I seem to glide, all spirit, my body the weight of a grain of sand. I pick up speed, flying fast, the darkness around burning into light. I am so quick, my movements so smooth, I don't make the slightest shadow fall. I can go anywhere, everywhere, see and know anything I want. Over a lake I become a fish; in the forest a matsutake, swelling in some dark and secret crack. I could even enter those big American men, swim into their minds and hearts.

But in the end, I always leave this blissful place, carrying my shadow, scratching my side. I want to feel the wetness of something sweet and sticky in my mouth. Such a disappointment, this fickle concentration, returning to the frail brown body, colander little mind. Why wish to love and be loved, then want this other life?

✍

I see myself in my apartment in California, a week or so from today, shaving my morning beard. Nong and Moua say, "Sisouphan, you, this philosophy, we do not understand." The razor moves across my cheek piling up the foam. Turning to the other side, I wonder, do Nong and Moua see these possibilities, such dreaming, this wanting, constant struggle, traversing this mind and heart? Maybe I hear them say, see this Sisouphan, pure as mountain air. Maybe I use the men who frighten me, Nong and Moua my friends, to grow big with pride. Perhaps I tell myself, this is the way of today, here in America, where I like to live.

This thing that holds those men who frighten me, pulling them taut and playing them like bamboo pipes of the *khene,* this ugly thing, is it fear? What is there to fear in America? That man's serrated voice, how did it get that way? Do they not wish to love like me? Yes, I think there is a reason the world needs us both, men like them and men like me. To see if we meet and touch, more and more each time, becoming bit by bit like the other. They do not see me put frogs in my mouth. I see their fear is close, safe and easy to clutch.

Surrounded by still trees in the forest, my stomach is grumbling loudly. I am hungry for the eggs in the brown paper bag, thirsty for the thermos tea. I miss Xana's fish paste. My *cafe au lait,* sweet rice-smelling Xana. I remember the way she looked that morning outside the restaurant, *mon Indochinoise,* folding a canna lily leaf into a triangular packet with my lunch inside.

I see a big one. A bulge like a woman's fist rising from the floor. It is ivory colored and magnificent, a matsutake mushroom. It smells of the baguette the street vendor sold in Luang Prabang. I dust the mud off of my mushroom and admire the skirt, the way it spreads. The money from this will buy a gift for Xana. She will smile, say "welcome back," smelling of colored rice.

"Stay strong in your head, my son, this is what you have." Sisouphan, I say quietly to myself, hold your breath and make your body wooden, drawing from the memory of that. Dreams, prayers, the struggle inside; this is part of love, the simple life. Nong and Moua and Xana, they leap around, here in America, trying to forget the past. I hoard my faith, my memories, like a squirrel hoards nuts. This treasure of mine, this is what helps Sisouphan be aware of Sisouphan in America. I hear the voice in my head say when I pray: *you stay still and grow this way. You stay still and watch.*

I am not doing so bad, my head hurts only a little. Such a pretty day, birds been saying all the time. For lunch in the woods, I knock this jumbo boiled egg on tree crotch.

Latha Viswanathan has worked as a journalist, copywriter, editor and teacher in India, London, Manila, Montreal, Toronto, and the United States. Her stories have appeared in major American literary magazines and won several awards. They have been published in *Best New Stories from the South* and broadcast on National Public Radio. She currently lives and writes in Houston